CAROLE WILKINSON

DRAGON KEEPER & DRAGON DAWN

D1313372

MACMILLAN CHILDREN'S BOOKS

First published in Australia 2008 by black dog books
Excerpts from *The Dragon Companion* (pp. 165–205) first published 2007 by
black dog books
First published in the UK 2009 by Macmillan Children's Books

This edition published 2010 by Macmillan Children's Books
a division of Macmillan Publishers Limited
20 New Wharf Road, London N1 9RR
Basingstoke and Oxford
Associated companies throughout the world
www.panmacmillan.com

ISBN 978-0-330-51003-5

JF

1 3 5 7 9 8 6 4 2

A CIP catalogue record for this book is available from
the British Library.

Printed and bound in the UK by CPI Mackays, Chatham ME5 8TD

DRAGON KEEPER
DRAGON DAWN

Carole Wilkinson was born in the UK but now lives in Melbourne, Australia, with her husband and daughter.

TO JOHN AND LILI
(AND RITA)

CONTENTS

Chapter One   WIDE AWAKE   1

Chapter Two   AT THE CROSSROADS   13

Chapter Three   AN UNFAITHFUL FRIEND   25

Chapter Four   CHICKEN AND PEARS   35

Chapter Five   A LEAP OF FAITH   51

Chapter Six   AMONG THE ASHES   63

Chapter Seven   OUTSIDE THE WALLS   77

Chapter Eight   THE DRAGONKEEPER'S HEIR   91

Chapter Nine   AN EMPTY STOMACH   107

Chapter Ten   A STRANGE SORT OF

                 RESCUE   117

Chapter Eleven   DREAMS AND SPLINTERS   127

Chapter Twelve   BATTLEGROUND   143

Glossary   157

Pronunciation   161

The Dragon Alphabet   165

Extract from DRAGONKEEPER: THE EDGE

   OF THE EMPIRE   207

ALL UNDER HEAVEN

LONG
WALL

QIN

Yangtze River

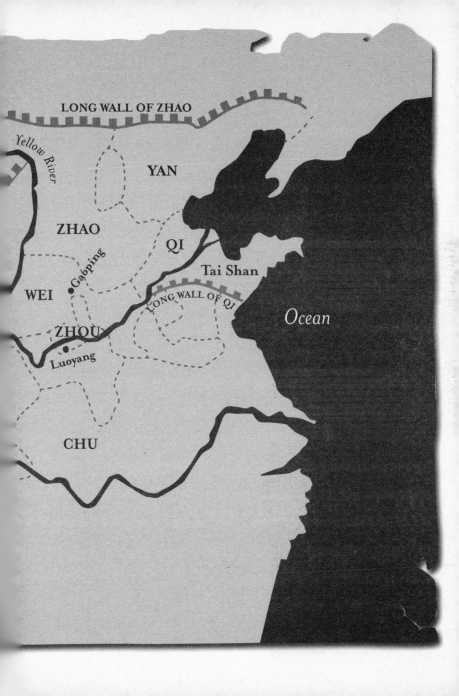

· CHAPTER ONE ·

WIDE AWAKE

It was a ghostly dawn. Fog, tinged with the faintest shade of pink, reduced the rising sun to a pale disc on the horizon. It brought no hope of warmth. In every direction the earth was covered with a carpet of white. The clouds were the same colour as the snow, and the fog made it impossible to see where the mountain peaks ended and the sky began. Ice crystals had formed a thin raft on the surface of a pool. One more night and it would freeze over.

Snowflakes settled on Danzi's nose. He had tried to convince himself that winter was still a long way off. He peered into the pool's depths. That's where he should have been. Down there. Asleep. A dragon should sleep through winter at the bottom of a pool. In the icy water he would enter a state of hibernation. His heart, lungs and liver would slow until they almost stopped. Glands on the side of his neck would extract a tiny amount of air from the water – just enough to survive. But hibernation didn't work for Danzi. It never had.

He'd tried counting bubbles as he sat on the bottom of the pool, but lost count somewhere beyond ten thousand. He'd tried reciting poetry – both his own and the lines of more celebrated poets. He'd imagined peaceful scenes of night falling, birds with their heads tucked under their wings, rabbits curled up in their burrows. It was no use. While other dragons slept, Danzi was still wide awake. At his last attempt, he'd tried humming a restful song – the one about the frog in the moon. He'd taken a deep breath ready to sing the chorus. A big mistake. He wasn't supposed to breathe while he was underwater, not in the regular way anyway. He'd swallowed a lot of water, and had to swim to the surface as fast as his four paws would allow.

Danzi walked over to a snow-covered mound. In previous years, the sleepless winters had passed quickly and pleasantly. He'd had the company of his Dragonkeeper, Chen-mo. They had sat around a cheerful fire, composing poetry, playing chess and reading from the one bamboo book that the Dragonkeeper had owned. This year, Danzi would spend the winter alone.

He'd enjoyed all his friendships with his human companions, but they were such frail creatures. Even if they survived wounds and didn't injure themselves in the mountains or succumb to one of the many human diseases, their lives were so short. No sooner did he get to know them, than he was burying them in the earth. Chen-mo had lived a long life, much longer than humans normally lived, but to Danzi it seemed like a brief time since they had first met.

There was one black shape in the landscape. It was the entrance to a cave. Inside, a nest of dried grass provided a bed where Danzi slept when he needed just a night's rest. It was also where he kept his winter food-store – dried mushrooms, berries, nuts – wrapped in bamboo leaves. Not a very appetizing selection, but all that was to be found on the bleak white peaks of Tai Shan. He went to the back of the cave and found his food packages had been gnawed open. Half-eaten nuts and mushrooms were scattered on the cave floor among rat droppings.

Rats. There was no creature Under Heaven that Danzi disliked more. Apart from centipedes, of course. Now that he hadn't the prospect of even a pawful of nuts or a dried mushroom to eat, he was suddenly very hungry. And there was only one thing that would satisfy his hunger – roasted bird. He decided to go down the mountain and catch a bird.

In fact, he would forget about hibernation entirely. He had an old friend who lived in the warmer south, a venerable tortoise whom he hadn't seen for two or three hundred years. He would visit the old crawler. Danzi felt pleased with himself. Dragons were known to be slow to make decisions, sometimes taking weeks. He'd just made three decisions before breakfast.

But before Danzi could start his journey to

somewhere where the sun was shining, there was one thing he had to do. He had promised to take his old Dragonkeeper's possessions to his family who lived in Gaoping, a village in the State of Wei. Chen-mo hadn't done his duty as a loyal son. He had abandoned his family to become a Dragonkeeper. His parents and even his brother would be long dead, but his nephews should still be alive. The old Dragonkeeper had feared that his souls wouldn't go to Heaven if he didn't make amends to his family.

Danzi reached up to a ledge hidden in the shadows and felt along it. He pulled down the Dragonkeeper's meagre possessions and took them outside into the light to inspect them. It wasn't much to show for a lifetime: a single gold coin, a small jade ornament in the shape of a winged horse, a bronze dagger and a circular mirror.

One side of the bronze mirror had a design etched into it — a dragon coiled around a raised sphere that acted as a knob or a handle. Danzi turned the mirror over. The other side was undecorated. He polished the tarnished surface on one of the tufts of hair that sprouted behind his knees and peered at his reflection.

He was a handsome dragon, if he did say so himself. His green scales glistened with melted snow. He'd lived through many adventures, but he bore few scars. His horns were both intact, his mane lustrous. The spines down his back were erect. His wings had grown early, well before the 1000 years that was usual for dragons. He was still a few years short of his first millennium.

There was no reason why Danzi must

have a human companion. It was just a custom, a habit that some dragons had acquired over the centuries – along with a taste for roasted birds, philosophical debate and pleasant music. He was a wild dragon, not one of those unfortunates who had been captured as a king's trophy or, worse still, bred in captivity never knowing freedom. He put the mirror back on the ledge. He didn't need another Dragonkeeper.

Danzi wrapped Chen-mo's possessions in a scrap of silk and walked over to the edge of a cliff. The snow was becoming heavier, but his tough overlapping scales didn't allow moisture to penetrate. Some snowflakes did find their way into his ears, however, which was annoying. He opened his wings and launched himself into the air, heading west.

Danzi soared higher and higher. It was hard work because he hadn't flown for a long while. In his final years, Chen-mo's fingers had become too arthritic to hold on to the dragon's mane as he flew. Instead, they had wandered the remote peaks of the Tai Shan mountain range on foot.

The clouds closed around Danzi like a damp, grey shroud. The cold penetrated his lungs, ice crystals formed on his wings, and the turbulence buffeted him as if he was an autumn leaf. He worked his wings harder, making deep, firm flaps.

He broke through the clouds and was bathed in sunlight. Gliding on a light breeze, the rays warmed his scales. He couldn't remember the last time he'd flown. He flapped his wings harder to gain speed, then suddenly dived down, startling an unsuspecting hawk. It felt good to be flying again. He soared up again and did a sideways roll. That would have been impossible to do with a human clinging on to his back. He executed a triple somersault. Then he had to glide again because he'd made himself dizzy.

Beyond the band of snow clouds, he could see soft green hills on the horizon. A good place to find a bird. That would be his first destination.

· CHAPTER TWO ·

AT THE CROSSROADS

irds were scarce so late in the year. It had taken Danzi almost all day to catch one. The tastiest birds were swallows, but they, along with most other birds, had flown south for the winter. He had managed to catch a scrawny pigeon, but had had to eat it raw. That was one reason he would miss having a Dragonkeeper. Danzi found it difficult to start a fire. His paws were dexterous, and he could work fire-making sticks fast enough to make a tuft of dried grass smoulder. But dragons were unable to purse their lips and their breath was misty and moist. That meant Danzi couldn't blow on the smouldering grass to make it catch fire.

Danzi had flown down to the flat lands where humans lived to rest his wings for a while. He had found a little-used track arched over with the bare branches of tallow trees. Although there was no snow, a cold wind was blowing. On such a dismal day most people would be indoors, but he had to be cautious. Humans could leap to all sorts of fanciful conclusions if they came across a dragon. They either saw it as a good omen and they wanted to bow down and make offerings, or they were convinced it was a bad omen, and were likely to chase him away. He didn't like having chinaberry sticks or bits of iron thrown at him – both were harmful to dragons. It was best to stay hidden from humans. Fortunately, dragons had a skill that enabled them to do that. They could shape-change.

The air around the dragon shimmered and shifted. His body appeared to waver and twist as if he was a mirage in a desert.

When the air regained its clarity, instead of a dragon, there stood an old man leaning on a walking stick.

Danzi was still hungry – hungry enough to consider snatching a chicken if he passed a farm. He'd leave a couple of copper coins in return for the bird, so it wouldn't be theft.

A babble of human voices broke into his contemplation of food. Up ahead, the trees thinned and the track crossed a main road. A group of men were huddled together at the crossroads. The babble became louder, rose to an excited shout and then died off in a disappointed groan. The men were gathered around a large flat stone that was covered with a red silk cloth. A young man placed three half walnut shells on the stone. He moved them around, so that the three shells were constantly changing place, first on the left, then the right, then the middle. He moved them in graceful loops, somehow managing to shift all three shells independently with just the tips of his fingers. The crowd of men watched, spellbound. Then the young man lifted one of the shells and put a small round pebble beneath it.

'Who's feeling lucky?' he asked as he resumed sliding the shells around smoothly and slowly. 'I'll wager five copper coins that no one can find the pebble.'

He glanced at a farmer carrying a basket of cabbages, who couldn't take his eyes off the swirling shells.

'You look like a lucky man, sir.' His voice was as hypnotic as the movements of the shells. 'Five copper coins if you can find the pebble. You've got nothing to lose.'

The shells stopped. The cabbage farmer pointed to one, and the young man lifted it. The pebble was underneath. The crowd cheered. The young man looked crestfallen as he handed over the five copper coins.

'My children will go hungry today,' he moaned. 'Let me have a chance to win back my cash. This time we'll make it double or nothing.'

The cabbage farmer licked his lips and put down his five copper coins. The young man placed the pebble under one of the shells. This time he moved them faster. But the farmer was confident. When the shells stopped, he immediately placed his finger on one of them. The young man lifted it up. The crowd groaned. There was nothing under it. He lifted one of the other shells and revealed the pebble. The cabbage farmer handed back the five copper coins and then fished in his pouch for another five.

Danzi, still in the shape of an old man, watched for some time. Men were lured into the game by the charming young man and left with their shoulders hunched and their money pouches lighter. None of the players ever won.

Like all dragons, Danzi's eyesight was exceptional. He could see the sleight of hand that fooled the unsuspecting players. He watched as more and more people fell for the trick. When a woman with two small children tried the game and lost what would have been money to feed her family, Danzi couldn't bear to watch any longer.

'Cheat!' he said to himself. Out of habit, he formed the words in his head using the language of humans, even though no one could hear them. 'Swindler!'

He strode towards the flat rock, slammed his walking stick down on it and swept the shells off. He snatched up the coins that the young man was about to pick up and held them out to the woman. The woman shrank back from Danzi's outstretched hand and let out a scream. She gathered up her children and ran off. The men in the crowd were all backing away with terrified expressions. Only the young trickster stayed calm.

Danzi looked down at his hand. It wasn't a human hand. The palm wasn't human flesh but the black satiny pads of an animal. The fingers weren't fingers at all but toes. The coins were caged by long, curved talons. Danzi's old man's arm was turning green and scaly. He had let his anger boil over. It was impossible for dragons to stay shape-changed when they were angry.

'You are nothing but a trickster!' Danzi said. He took deep breaths to calm himself. His paw took on the form of a human hand again.

The young man took the coins. 'Even tricksters have to eat,' he said, searching for his scattered shells.

The fact that the old man's hand had turned green and changed into a paw hadn't disturbed him at all.

'That woman will have difficulty enough feeding her children through the winter,' Danzi said, 'without you taking her money.'

The trickster was about to speak again, but then looked over his shoulder as if he'd heard something. His self-confident smile disappeared. Two soldiers were further down the road, demanding to see travel permits. They grabbed one of the men who had been playing the shell game and tied his hands behind him. The trickster quickly packed up his shells and his cloth, and ran – not along the road but into the trees. It wasn't until after he'd disappeared that Danzi wondered if the man could have heard his thoughts.

Blue pennants fluttered from the soldiers' spears. Danzi guessed that they were recruiting for the Wei army. That was why the young man had disappeared so quickly. No one was allowed to travel without a permit. Any man without a permit would be arrested and conscripted into the army. Danzi's old-man shape was too elderly to be of interest to the soldiers, but he didn't want to risk getting caught up in the conflicts of men. He shuffled away until he was out of sight, then he changed into a hawk and flew off.

It was a bad time to be travelling through the world of humans. There was war. Danzi had hoped that the fighting would have ceased during winter, but it seemed he was wrong.

· CHAPTER THREE ·

AN UNFAITHFUL FRIEND

D anzi woke from a deep sleep. Something was raining down on him. It wasn't drops of water, but clods of earth. He had been sleeping in a hollow he'd dug to protect himself from the early-morning chill. Something sharp was sticking into his side. He shielded his eyes with one paw to stop the dirt getting into them. There was a bone lying beside him. It looked like a well-chewed leg of pork. He sat up and peered over the edge of his hollow and was confronted by a large, hairy rump. A sandy-coloured dog was digging up earth with its front paws and shovelling it between its legs into the hole.

Danzi made a deep rumbling sound like someone beating a large metal drum. The dog leaped off the ground, spun around in midair and landed shivering in fear.

'Stupid beast!' Danzi roared. 'Did you not see me sleeping here?'

The dog put its tail between its legs and whimpered. It had probably never seen a dragon before. It certainly couldn't understand what the dragon was saying, but it knew that he was angry. Danzi climbed out of the hollow, brushed the dirt off his scales and tried to pat the dog on the head. It shrank away from him.

Danzi made tinkling sounds like wind chimes in a gentle breeze, to show the dog that he wasn't going to attack it. 'I will not hurt you. You startled me.'

He stroked the dog's sandy fur. Its tail quivered tentatively. Danzi took a package from the hollow and sat down on a log. The dog watched as he unwrapped the leaves that protected his food. All Danzi had for breakfast was one mushroom and a few nuts.

The dog fetched its bone and put it at the dragon's feet.

'Are you offering to share your bone with me?'

The dog wagged its tail. It was a very meaty bone. Danzi sliced off a chunk of pork with a talon.

'I am most grateful.'

While he ate the meat, the dog chewed on the end of the bone.

Danzi felt much better with something in his stomach. He stood up and scratched an itch on his tail. The muscles in his wings were sore after his long flight the previous day, so he decided to walk for a while. The dog trotted alongside him with the bone in its mouth. The morning couldn't have been more pleasant. The air was crisp, but the sky had cleared and the sun warmed him. The snow-peaked mountains looked delightful – now that they were in the distance. There were just a few leaves clinging to the branches. Danzi enjoyed swishing through the red and yellow leaves that carpeted the path. He began to compose a poem and wished he had a brush and a piece of calfskin to write on. He would just have to commit it to memory.

The dog padded alongside him, tongue hanging out, a toothy smile on its face, tail erect. Danzi glanced between the dog's legs. It was a male. He would make a pleasant companion – one who would never disagree with him, which would make a change. Humans could be argumentative, and his last Dragonkeeper had been very opinionated.

The dog might be a useful hunter, or at least a retriever when Danzi used a slingshot to bring down birds and rabbits. A dragon couldn't get a human to do that!

'The only trouble would be when it came to flying,' Danzi said.

The dog suddenly stopped, sat down and scratched himself.

'That explains my itchy tail,' Danzi thought. 'The dog has given me fleas!'

Danzi was staring at the branches over-head, trying to think of an adjective to describe the way the sunlight shone through the leaves, when a faint whistling sound startled him. Like all dragons, Danzi's hearing wasn't good so he couldn't make out where the sound was coming from. The dog knew. He crouched low, and Danzi shape-changed into a bush just before a man came over the crest of a hill. The man put his fingers to his mouth and whistled long and loud enough for Danzi to hear.

It seemed the man was looking for his lost dog . . . and perhaps his lost ham bone as well.

'Ungrateful animal!' the man called. 'If you don't come here right away, I'll . . .' The man's voice trailed away as he realized that the threat of a beating wasn't the best way to lure a wayward dog.

'You are not homeless at all!' Danzi said. 'Go to your master!'

The dog stared at the bush with his head cocked to one side. He was still sitting there when the man found him

'You bad dog,' he said. 'Come here.'

The dog slunk towards his master.

'And since you're so fond of pork,' the

man said, as he tied a length of rope around the dog's neck, 'you can sleep with the pigs tonight!'

The man set off home, pulling the reluctant dog behind him.

Danzi made a soft sound, like a cracked bell ringing in the distance, as sadness settled on his heart.

He decided it was not a good plan to walk while he was so close to human habitation. He took to the air again.

CHAPTER FOUR

CHICKEN AND PEARS

It was perfect flying weather. Danzi had been aloft all morning. The sun warmed his back and the breeze was in his favour. Fluffy white clouds hung below him, providing enough cover so that he didn't have to shape-change. From below he would be seen only as a fleeting dark shape between the clouds, easily mistaken for a large bird. But as he peered through the spaces Danzi could see the whole landscape below.

It was a shame the dog hadn't been able to stay. Dogs devoted themselves to their masters for life. Humans preferred to think of themselves as the masters. And they had a tendency to injure themselves – physically and emotionally. If they weren't falling down crevices, they were falling in love. He had made the right decision. He was better off without a Dragonkeeper.

He pondered alternative companions – a pangolin perhaps or a monkey, but they were wild beasts and hard to tame. Pandas were placid creatures, but they had to spend most of the day eating bamboo leaves in order to get the nutrition they needed. With a panda as a companion, he'd never be able to get anywhere. Then there was the problem of transportation. Danzi wasn't sure he'd be able to get off the ground with a full-grown panda on his back.

Ducks and storks flew overhead in straggly arrowhead formations, on their way south for the winter. A bird might make a pleasant companion (though it would have to be a large one that he wouldn't be tempted to eat if he got hungry). It would have sharp hearing and it could fly alongside him, only perching on his back when it needed a rest.

But he didn't want to be forever cleaning bird droppings off his scales.

He would have to get used to travelling alone again, even though it was a little boring. His last Dragonkeeper had had a good sense of humour and they had enjoyed playing jokes on each other. One of Danzi's favourite jokes was to shape-change into something while Chen-mo wasn't looking. Then he would have to work out if the dragon had turned into a bush or a rock or a log. It was even more fun in a town. The challenge was to shape-change at the split second when no one was watching. The Dragonkeeper would then have to guess whether Danzi had changed into a small child or a dog or a sack of grain. It was hilarious when the man found himself mistakenly speaking to a wine jar.

Danzi was flying above a plain in the State of Zhou. It was good farming land. There were many villages, and every foot of land had been turned into fields. The buildings looked tiny, like models made to be buried with the dead. The sun glinted on small ponds and dams, so that they looked like jewels dropped by a careless Heavenly princess.

He would have to fly in his hawk shape as much as possible to avoid being seen. There were humans who hunted dragons. It was best to be cautious. But flying while shape-changed took a great deal of concentration and energy. The more he flew, the more rest he would need. Danzi's wing muscles were strengthening and he was pleased with his progress so far. He was only just starting to tire, even though he had flown further than on previous days. It was still several hours until sunset, but after so many hours flying in his hawk shape, he was ready for a rest.

There was a village directly below him, the usual huddle of ten or fifteen houses surrounded by a mud-brick wall. Outside the wall were fields of green vegetables and wheat. The villagers were out in the fields cutting and threshing their grain. Danzi circled down and perched on the village wall. There was a mouth-watering smell in the air. Danzi sniffed. Stewed duck and turnips if he wasn't mistaken.

Two boys were playing a game with sticks and a block of wood. They had marked a large square in the dust and were each trying to hit their block out of the square, while preventing the other from doing the same.

One of them looked up at the bird on the wall. Danzi couldn't help himself – when the boy glanced away he turned into a vase. The boy looked back and his mouth dropped open.

'Did you see that?'

'What?' his friend asked.

'There was a big bird on the wall and it just turned into a vase.'

The boy pointed to the top of the wall, but while the child had been talking, Danzi had changed back into a hawk.

'Looks like a bird to me,' the other boy said. 'You just said that to distract me so that you could cheat!'

'Did not!'

'Did!'

The two boys started to scuffle in the dust. Danzi chuckled to himself. He flew off in his hawk shape to the villagers' orchard. He had no food with him, but there were several late-fruiting pear trees covered with deep red leaves. He changed back to his true form, picked six or seven of the juicy pears and ate two of them, core and all.

'We meet again.'

Danzi started as he turned towards the voice. A young man was standing under one of the pear trees, leaning up against the coarse bark with his arms folded. It was the trickster he'd seen at the crossroads.

'Where did you come from?' Danzi was shocked that the man had been able to sneak up on him so easily.

'I fancied a pear for my supper, just like you.'

The young man looked Danzi up and down. Danzi felt uncomfortable. He wasn't used to being in his true shape in full view of a human he didn't know. The young man studied the dragon with interest – his horns, his whiskers, the end of his tail. He didn't seem at all flustered to be confronted by a full-grown dragon.

'You can hear the words I speak in my mind,' Danzi said.

The young man began collecting twigs and dry grass. 'Can't everyone?'

He arranged the twigs in a small heap, pulled out some firesticks, and before long he had a fire going. He dug into his bag and produced a dead chicken, which he proceeded to pluck. Then he skewered it on a stick and laid it on the coals. Soon the smell of roasting bird was drifting into Danzi's nostrils and making his stomach rumble.

'Would you like to join me for supper?' the trickster asked.

'I am not hungry,' Danzi replied. He didn't trust the trickster. 'I have already eaten.'

'Two pears isn't much of a meal for a mature dragon. I'm sure you could find room for more.'

Danzi's mouth was watering. 'Did you steal it?'

'I took it when no one was looking . . . just the same as you did those pears.'

Danzi looked guiltily at the other pears lying at his feet.

'As winter approaches, there's only so much food to share around,' the young man said. 'Someone always goes hungry. Sometimes it's me . . . but not tonight.'

He calmly poked the coals with a stick,

as if he chatted with a dragon every other day. Danzi watched him. The young man held the stick in his right hand. In his long life, the only humans Danzi had come across who could hear his dragon voice in their mind were Dragonkeepers. These were rare people, descended from just two families – either the Huan or Yu families. Dragonkeepers possessed three particular characteristics – left-handedness was one of them.

'What is your name?' Danzi asked.

'Fang,' the man said. 'Fang Bingwen. And what is your name?'

'I am Long Danzi.'

'Do you travel alone?'

'Yes. I do not need a companion.'

When the chicken was cooked, Fang Bingwen pulled the bird in two and handed half to Danzi. The dragon accepted it. They ate in silence and then shared the pears.

'Did you follow me?' Danzi asked.

'Why would I do that?' Bingwen replied. 'You are too clever to fall for my tricks.'

'How else would you happen to cross my path twice?'

'I could just as easily ask how you come to cross my path,' Bingwen replied. 'I have been to this village before. I tricked the elder into parting with a string of cash. Last night I had a dream that I came back.'

Danzi felt his anger rising again. 'You seem proud of your dishonesty.'

Bingwen shrugged. 'I make a good living.'

'You are a fraud.'

'You trick humans too,' Bingwen said.

'Only for their own good.'

'What about the boy in the village?' asked Bingwen.

'That was a harmless joke. I was not taking the food from his mouth.'

'What about the pears?'

'I do not make a living out of stealing from people. I only do it when I have no choice.' Bingwen threw sticks on the fire. It flared up. Danzi was getting hot. He moved back from the fire. Bingwen's anger had flared up with the fire. 'It's only greedy people that imagine they can get something for nothing who take up my wager.'

Danzi was about to argue when he noticed something glint among the black tree trunks. Two soldiers stepped out of the shadows into the firelight, swords drawn. Danzi was outside the circle of firelight. He moved further into the darkness and shape-changed into a bush. Bingwen jumped to his feet, grabbed his bag and ran – straight into another four soldiers.

One of the soldiers looked around. 'Where's the other one? You were talking to someone.'

'There's nobody else,' Bingwen said. 'I was talking to myself.'

Danzi took to the skies. His night vision was good. He circled in the darkness and watched as the soldiers bound Bingwen's hands and marched him away. Bingwen didn't resist. There was no point. One against six were not good odds.

CHAPTER FIVE

A LEAP OF FAITH

Danzi stayed in the pear orchard until morning. It was the one place he knew he'd be safe. The soldiers would not return. He didn't sleep though. The soldiers who had taken Bingwen away were from the State of Qin; Danzi knew that from their blue and red uniforms. There was a time when the Qin were nothing but a ragged bunch of mountain men. But the man who had become their king had turned them into a formidable force. From their mountain stronghold in the west, they had swept down to attack the smaller states. Now they were invading Zhou.

The Qin didn't just conscript their own citizens into their army, they conscripted foreigners. The smaller states kept enemy prisoners as slaves, but didn't trust them with weapons in case they used them on their captors. The Qin had solved the problem. In battle, they put all their foreign conscripts in the frontline, using them as a human shield to protect their own soldiers. They left the captives in their peasant dress or in their own uniforms if they were soldiers. That made the enemy hesitate before they fired, giving the Qin bowmen plenty of time to shower arrows on them.

Danzi took off into a grey sky. He needed to get out of the reach of the Qin soldiers as soon as possible. They knew the value of a dragon. He would be a handsome prize to offer their king. He tried to fly through the clouds, but they were too thick. Buffeted back and forth, blown up and down by the turbulence, he was forced to fly beneath the clouds and take the shape of a hawk again.

He couldn't get his mind off Bingwen. He should have rescued the young man, even though he was a cheat. He could have swooped down, dug his talons into his jacket and carried him off.

'He is not my concern,' Danzi told himself as he flapped on through steady rain.

Bingwen had been travelling without a permit in a time of war. He must have known what would happen if he was caught. He should have chosen an honest living and stayed in his home with his family as all good sons should.

After just a couple of hours in flight, Danzi was already in need of a rest. He hadn't had any sleep the previous night so it wasn't surprising that he was weary. If he slept for an hour or two, he would be refreshed – and the rain might have stopped by then.

Danzi could see a range of low hills beneath him. In his hawk shape, he flew lower, searching for a secluded spot. A ruined tower sat on the top of one of the hills, overlooking a chasm. It was a three-storey lookout post, or at least it had been. Built in another time, by another army, it had long been abandoned. The roof had disappeared and the top floor was exposed to the sky.

A herd of goats was grazing on the slopes beneath the tower. They all looked up as Danzi approached, but didn't find the sight of a hawk alarming, and went back to nibbling the grass. The goatherd was sheltering from the rain against the southern wall of the tower, where he had set up a blanket to form a tent with his staff and a tree branch. Danzi flew to the other side of the tower where the wall had crumbled away almost entirely, leaving the rooms open to the elements. Danzi glided into the second-storey room. Most of the ceiling was still intact, and there were windows in the remaining walls so that he could see in all directions. He settled down to rest.

He was dreaming about a group of drummers beating their drum skins when he woke. What in his dreams had been the pounding of drums was in fact the thunder of goat hooves. He went over to one of the windows. Goats were running in panic around the tower. A company of Qin soldiers had chosen that very hillside for an encampment. They had probably thought it would be a good vantage point, just as

Danzi had. It was also a good source of food. Several of the goats were being butchered for the soldiers to eat.

The goatherd was held captive and he wasn't the only prisoner. There were at least a dozen men lined up with their hands tied behind them. A captain was shouting orders at them, raising his sword to show his authority. Only one man refused to do as he was told. Danzi recognized him. It was Bingwen. The dragon had slept much longer than he'd thought if they'd had time to catch up with him.

The captain hit Bingwen with the hilt of his sword, knocking him to the ground. The soldier then dragged the young man to his knees and held the sword blade at his throat. But Bingwen was not ready to die. With a twist of his wrists, he managed to free his hands and knock the sword from the captain's hand. Bingwen turned to run, but the entire company had heard their captain's cry of anger. Across the hillside, soldiers were reaching for their swords and loading their crossbows. Bingwen had no choice. The only way he could run was up the hill to the tower.

Danzi took to the skies in his hawk shape and circled above the tower. The top of the hill was rocky and steep. When Bingwen reached the foot of the crumbling tower, he stood panting. Soldiers were advancing towards him. He went round to the other side of the tower. Just a narrow strip of land was left where a section of the hilltop had collapsed and shorn off, leaving a steep drop of more than ten *chang*.

Bingwen climbed the steps to the roof

of the tower. He stood on the edge of the top storey and looked down at the rocks far below. Several soldiers were only a few steps behind him, swords ready to hack him to death. He was cornered.

Danzi swooped low, changing back to his dragon shape as he did. He let out a roar. The first soldiers had already reached the top of the tower. They stared up at the green dragon. Danzi didn't have time to land and take off again.

He glided as close to the tower as he could without clipping his wing on the crumbling mud bricks, but he was still two or three *chang* away from Bingwen.

'Jump on my back!' He formed the words in his mind.

The young man didn't hesitate. He leaped off the tower and hurled himself towards the dragon. He would have made it, but a volley of arrows streaked into the air and Danzi was forced to weave sideways to avoid them. Bingwen fell short. He hit Danzi's flank, clawing at the dragon's scales, but he couldn't get a hold. He slid off.

Danzi twisted back. He saw the look in Bingwen's eyes as the young man fell. It was the look of someone who was not ready to die. He grasped the back of Bingwen's jacket in his talons. The fabric was old and worn. It began to tear. Bingwen reached up and grabbed hold of the tuft of hair on the back of Danzi's leg. The jacket ripped through and Bingwen swung one-handed.

Danzi wove to avoid more arrows, but Bingwen clung on. The dragon flexed his foot and the young man swung his leg over it and then was able to grasp a handful of

Danzi's mane and haul himself up on to the dragon's back. Danzi didn't have time to wait until Bingwen was safely seated. He flapped his wings hard. Another volley of arrows arced into the sky, but Danzi was already out of range.

· CHAPTER SIX ·

AMONG THE ASHES

anzi circled over a marshy area, looking for somewhere to land. When he did, he dropped Bingwen on the soggy ground.

The young man was smiling, despite the fact that he had just been close to death.

'That was wonderful,' he whispered.

'Nearly ending up as a conscript in the Qin army?'

'No. Flying,' Bingwen said. 'I've never experienced anything like it. Seeing All Under Heaven spread beneath me . . .' He sighed. 'It's so beautiful.'

Bingwen was still lying on the ground, staring at the sky as if he wished he was back up there again.

'I am delighted that you enjoyed the flight,' Danzi said crossly, 'but do not expect me to rescue you again.'

Humans were a nuisance. Danzi had had enough of them. If it hadn't been for his promise to his dying Dragonkeeper, he would have been heading as far away from human habitation as possible. He was tired, more tired than he would have expected to be after a short flight with one skinny passenger.

Bingwen stood up and dusted off his jacket. 'Where are you going?'

'I am going to the village of Gaoping,' Danzi replied. 'Then, after I have fulfilled a promise to an old friend, I am going to find somewhere more peaceful.'

'I'd like to get away from those soldiers. Could you take me to Gaoping? I can pay.'

'I do not want your stolen money,' Danzi snapped.

'Please, just one more short flight.'

'I will take you on one condition.'

Bingwen waited.

'You must give up your dishonest trade and find yourself some decent employment.'

Bingwen nodded. He climbed up on to the dragon's back before he had any chance to object.

They flew for some time. The silence was broken by the rush of the wind and Bingwen's frequent exclamations at the wonderful sights that lay below him.

'You are either very brave or very foolhardy,' Danzi said, 'leaping off the tower the way you did.'

'I had no other choice. I know what the Qin do with their captives.'

Danzi didn't want to admit it, but he was impressed by the trickster's courage.

Gaoping appeared on the horizon. Danzi cried out. It was a terrible sound like someone banging copper bowls together. Bingwen had to cover his ears. He peered into the distance.

'What's wrong? What do you see?'

Danzi didn't answer.

Soon the smoke was visible even to human eyes. Gaoping had been burned to the ground. Danzi circled over the smoking village and then landed among the ashes. Bingwen climbed down and saw what Danzi's dragon eyes had already seen. There were bodies everywhere. Headless bodies. And there was a horrible smell. It was burnt flesh. The blood drained from Bingwen's face. His legs became unsteady. He leaned against Danzi to stop himself from falling.

'Who did this?' Bingwen whispered.

'There is only one army that beheads their enemies – the Qin. The soldiers collect the heads of their victims. If they have enough, they are promoted.'

'But these poor people were just villagers. Why did they kill them?'

'An invading army strips the land of food like locusts,' Danzi replied. 'The villagers must have tried to defend their animals and their store of grain. It was foolish.'

'But if they'd let the Qin take their food, they would have died of hunger over winter anyway.'

Danzi nodded sadly.

Bingwen was searching through the burnt remains. He picked up a shard of a broken bowl, a rake with its handle burned away, a blackened doll.

'You will find nothing of value here,'

Danzi snapped. 'These were poor people.'

Bingwen turned to the dragon. The smoke and the wind-blown ashes had blackened his face. Tears were making pathways through the grime. Danzi wished he hadn't spoken so sharply. He had assumed that the young man was looking for something valuable that had survived the flames. The dragon and the young man walked through the ruined village hoping to find survivors. There were none.

The charred remains of the simple houses were like a row of black and broken teeth. Not one was left whole. Danzi wondered which house Chen-mo's family had lived in. Now he wouldn't be able to fulfill his promise to his old Dragonkeeper.

'The violence of humans sickens me,' he said.

'Don't dragons ever fight?'

'Yes, dragons fight, but it is only ever one dragon pitted against another, and a dragon fight rarely ends in death.'

There were too many dead to bury. Danzi found an altar, scorched but still standing. He picked some leaves from a nearby camphor tree and burned them on the altar.

'We have nothing to give as an offering to Heaven,' Danzi said.

The dragon and the young man stood in the blackened silence. Then Bingwen took a breath and began to sing. It was a melancholy tune, a song to the dead. The clear notes of his song drifted up with the fragrant smoke. Danzi hoped the ancestors of the dead would smell the smoke, hear the singing and guide the villagers' souls to

Heaven. The lengthening shadows turned the burnt village from sad to sinister.

'We've done everything we can for the souls of the dead,' Bingwen said.

'Only for the souls that start the perilous journey to Heaven soon after death. There are still the earth-bound souls. Without proper graves and their families to attend them, those souls will turn into angry ghosts,' said Danzi.

Bingwen shivered. 'There will be a lot of angry ghosts here.'

Danzi wanted to leave immediately, but he didn't have the energy to fly far.

'I used to be able to fly all day without getting tired, but lately even short flights wear me out,' he complained.

'We can spend the night in the fields outside the village,' Bingwen said.

The Qin soldiers had stripped the fields of their crops, but the young man was an experienced scavenger. He found a bruised squash, three onions and some limp greens. He had some grain in his bag. He lit a fire and, with the addition of some herbs that were growing nearby, he soon had a surprisingly fragrant meal cooking. Danzi had nothing to contribute to the meal. He sank down next to the fire and accepted with thanks when Bingwen offered to share the small meal with him.

'Would you like a game of chess?' Bingwen asked after they had eaten. 'It might take our minds off the horrors we have seen.'

Danzi was tired, but he welcomed the idea of some activity. Bingwen took out his red cloth. On the reverse side, a chessboard was marked. He placed some tiny chess pieces on the cloth. One set was made of green jade and carved in the shape of bears. The other was white jade and shaped like tigers.

'That is a handsome chess set,' Danzi said.

'My family were jade carvers.'

'Why did you not join your family business?'

Bingwen moved a chess piece. Danzi could tell he didn't like talking about his past.

'It's a long story.'

Danzi made his move. 'We have hours to pass before dawn.'

'My family was unlucky. We lived in a village in the mountains where everyone made their living from carving jade. My grandfather was the finest jade carver. His work was sought by kings. Then one day, when my father was still a boy, Grandfather walked off to live in the mountains. My father and his brother were forced to support the family. It was hard work. Father was not a skilled carver. He had to work in the jade mines.'

Now the young man had started to tell his story, he couldn't stop. Danzi wondered if it was a trick to distract him from the game.

'Father was convinced the family was cursed. His brother left the village to get other work. Father vowed he would never marry and have children. He met my mother when he was old. He thought they were too old to have children, but he was wrong. My mother died in childbirth. Father had to continue to work in the jade mines. He put me in the care of Master Fang and his wife.'

Bingwen lost the game and then curled up in his blanket near the fire without another word.

Danzi found it hard to sleep so close to the destroyed village. Whenever he closed his eyes, he saw the dead of Gaoping. He could feel the presence of the wretched souls of the villagers. They cried out in anguish, confusion and despair, but they were too new to death to be angry yet. The dead did not trouble them during the night.

· CHAPTER SEVEN ·

OUTSIDE THE WALLS

When Bingwen woke, he didn't mention the horrors of the previous day – or the story he had told about his family.

'I had such strange dreams,' he said as he built a small fire and put on a pot of water to heat.

'What sort of dreams?' Danzi asked.

Bingwen didn't answer him. 'We have no food.' He was searching through his bag. 'But I have something to flavour the water. It will be better than nothing.' He threw a handful of sweet herbs and dried berries into the pot and watched it boil. Then he poured out a bowl of the hot drink and gave it to Danzi.

'Where will you go now?' Danzi asked.

'Somewhere beyond the reach of the Qin.' Bingwen sipped his drink. 'Since you are heading south—'

'I am not going south now,' Danzi interrupted.

'I thought you were going to find a place with a warmer climate?'

'My plan has changed. I am weary. I will return to Tai Shan and try to hibernate. If that is not possible, I must at least rest. I do not have enough energy for adventure.'

Bingwen was silent for a moment.

'But you'll need supplies to see you through the winter, won't you?'

The dragon nodded.

'And I'll need supplies for my journey as well,' Bingwen said. He paused. 'How far are we from the city of Luoyang?'

'Perhaps 300 *li*.'

'We should go there and get provisions.'

Danzi looked at the young man

suspiciously, trying to guess his thoughts.

'Don't worry. Once I have supplies, I won't trouble you with my presence any longer.' Bingwen looked at the weary dragon. 'How long is it since you had a decent meal?'

'It has been a long time.'

'I think you need a dragon-sized meal before the winter.'

Danzi couldn't argue with that. It was customary for dragons to eat well before they hibernated.

By choosing a route over unpopulated areas, the dragon didn't have to shape-change. Bingwen held on to the dragon's mane and flew without fear. Danzi had never had a rider who was as comfortable without a harness.

'You are lucky to have wings,' Bingwen

shouted over the rush of wind. 'I love the way you can see how the land crumples up into mountains and the river slips smoothly around them like liquid silver. People lose their significance; they become invisible.'

An expanse of water appeared below them, dimpled by the wind. There was just one tiny wisp of cloud that had been left behind. Bingwen pointed to a sharp ridge of mountains that pierced the air, the peaks covered with snow.

'A mountain is so immovable, so proud, so grand,' he said. 'You feel you have to be silent in its presence, bow your head. All Under Heaven is so ordered. Look at those birds.' He pointed to a flock of geese, honking noisily as they flapped their way south.

'I would be most grateful if you would hold on with both hands,' Danzi interrupted.

'Sorry,' Bingwen said. 'Those birds never consider whether their lives are worth living or not. They obey their Heaven-given instincts. They collect food, they mate and lay eggs, they fly south for the winter. Every creature has its place in the world. Butterflies, bamboo and bluebirds all live out their allotted time on earth as Heaven decrees.'

'And what about you?' Danzi asked. 'What has Heaven decreed for you?'

Bingwen didn't answer.

It was a long, slow flight and Danzi had to stop to rest many times. They reached Luoyang late in the afternoon. There were enough clouds so that in the dying light

Danzi could risk circling over the city in his dragon shape.

The Zhou capital had seen better times. The walls of Luoyang were crumbling, the houses unpainted, the palace in disrepair. Danzi could remember a time when Zhou was the most powerful state Under Heaven.

'The city's preparing for an attack,' Bingwen said. 'They must have heard about the destruction of Gaoping.'

The gates were well guarded. Soldiers were positioning themselves on the walls. A dozen men were dragging a huge crossbow up to the battlements.

'They will need more than that to withstand the Qin,' Danzi said.

Outside the city walls, a commander was drilling new recruits. The men had no uniforms and some were wielding wooden sticks instead of swords. The commander barked orders and the recruits turned in different directions, bumping into each other and dropping their weapons. The dragon touched down outside the city walls, taking cover in a clump of bamboo.

'We have just enough time to enter the city before nightfall.'

'Wouldn't it be easier to fly into the city at night?' Bingwen asked. 'The darkness will hide you.'

The sun was low in the sky. A light wind was blowing away the remaining clouds.

'It will be a clear night,' Danzi replied. 'A dragon's scales absorb moonlight. Tonight's moon will be almost full. I would light up like a lantern.'

'So how will we get in?' Bingwen asked.

'We can't just walk through the gate. The guards will be checking everyone's permits.'

'I can shape-change into a bat,' Danzi replied.

'What about me?'

Danzi would need Bingwen to make purchases in the city. He thought for a moment.

'I will change into something that will lure the guards away from the gate, so that you can sneak in.'

'What shape will you take?'

Danzi made a slow clinking sound, like someone lightly striking a metal bowl with a spoon, as he considered his options. So late in the day, he couldn't rely on the guards to be alert enough to notice a bush jumping from one spot to another. A sack of gold from a distance looked no different to a sack of grain.

'I think I have the right shape in mind,' he said finally. 'Check that there is no one on the road.'

Bingwen peered up and down the road. There was no one in sight. When he turned back, he saw a lovely woman emerge from the bamboo grove. The young man stared at her flawless skin and her hair, which was elegantly coiled on top of her head and held in place by a silver comb. 'Is that you, Danzi?'

The woman nodded and walked towards the gate. Then she stopped suddenly and looked around on the ground. Bingwen wasn't sure what he was supposed to do, but he was an expert at deception. He got down on his hands and knees as if he was looking for something. The lovely woman soon caught the eye of the guards and they both came running over.

'My mistress has lost her necklace,' Bingwen said. 'It was a present from the King of Zhou himself!'

The guards looked at the woman again, no doubt wondering who this important woman was. Tears were welling in her eyes.

'We'll help you look for it, madam,' one of the guards said, immediately dropping to his knees.

'When do you think you might have lost it?' the other asked.

'She is sure she felt it against her neck just a short while ago,' Bingwen said. He was enjoying his performance. 'Perhaps if you search back the way we came.'

The guards obediently walked back along the road, head down, searching for the missing necklace in the fading light.

Bingwen smiled at their diligence, then he turned and ran off in the other direction – into the city.

'You might have to wait till morning,' one of the guards said. 'It's too dark to . . .'

He looked around for the young woman. 'Where'd she go?'

There was no sign of her or her servant. The guards took no notice of the bat flapping over the city walls.

CHAPTER EIGHT

THE DRAGONKEEPER'S HEIR

ack in his old-man shape, Danzi led Bingwen to an inn that he knew from a previous visit to Luoyang, but it had been commandeered as a barracks for soldiers. It was the same at three other inns they tried. Bingwen finally found an old widow who was happy to give them a room.

'Don't you have any baggage?' the widow asked, peering behind them as if expecting to see a servant laden with bags.

'No,' Bingwen replied. 'It will be following tomorrow . . . by carriage.'

The widow had given them her own sleeping quarters. It was a simple, clean room, but there was only one narrow bed.

'We paid a very high price for such a small room,' Danzi grumbled, once the woman had left them.

'It's the best we can hope for at a time like this,' Bingwen said. 'Our host will be sleeping on the kitchen floor.'

The widow had agreed to cook them a meal and when it was ready Bingwen brought the food to the small room and spread it out on a low table. Danzi breathed in the aroma. It was indeed a long time since he'd had a hearty meal. It was not a time of plenty in Luoyang, but the woman had done her best with what ingredients she could buy with the money Bingwen had given her. There was pigeon in jackal broth, pickled pork, millet and a sour salad, as well as wine and dried jujubes.

When they had finished eating, Bingwen took the empty bowls to the kitchen, and Danzi collapsed on the bed. It groaned under his weight, but held up. When Bingwen returned, he found the dragon was asleep. He took the blanket and made his bed on the floor.

When Danzi woke, Bingwen had already ordered breakfast and was making a shopping list for the supplies they would need.

'Bingwen, I cannot—'

'I understand. You don't want to be hampered by a troublesome human.' Bingwen held up his hand to stop Danzi interrupting. 'From here we will go our separate ways.'

Danzi didn't feel at all rested, despite a good night's sleep.

'You stay here,' Bingwen said. 'I'll find the market and buy the food.'

Danzi didn't argue. He couldn't understand why he felt so tired. He decided it must have been because of all the shape-changing he'd been doing. It was a skill he hadn't used very much over the past years.

Bingwen returned with a basket of nuts, dried fruit, millet and onions.

'There is no reason to linger in this city,' Danzi said.

'No,' Bingwen agreed, 'but I think we should leave from the west gate, in case the guards recognize me from yesterday.'

Danzi couldn't argue with his logic, but as he followed Bingwen through the city streets, he wasn't sure that they were heading in the right direction.

Bingwen stopped outside a woodcarver's workshop to put down his bag for a moment and rest. The woodcarver was busy carving arrows and, from the pile of arrows at his side, it looked like he'd been up all night trying to meet the needs of the Zhou army.

'What did you say your Dragonkeeper's family name was?' Bingwen asked.

'Huan,' Danzi replied, though he couldn't remember ever mentioning it.

Bingwen was pointing to a sign. It proclaimed the superior woodcarving skills of Master Huan.

Danzi looked at the sign and then at the woodcarver bent over his work. Master Huan called to a boy aged about seven, who was asleep on a sack in the corner. The boy got up and began to fit trimmed feathers to the arrows. Bingwen had already struck up a conversation with the woodcarver. Before long, he had established that he had once lived in Gaoping.

'What a coincidence!' Bingwen said. 'I

think you must be the man we are looking for.'

'I left that village years ago,' Master Huan said, wiping the sweat from his face and looking at the strangers with suspicion.

'It's lucky that you did leave,' Bingwen said. 'The Qin have attacked it and left a burning ruin.'

'Yes, news reached us about the massacre at Gaoping. That's why we're preparing for war.' He peered at the strangers. 'Why were you looking for me? I'm too old to be conscripted, and my boy is too young.'

'Our arrival has nothing to do with the war, Master Huan.' Bingwen pointed to Danzi. 'This venerable gentleman was a good friend of your uncle.'

Master Huan's frown deepened. 'I don't have an uncle.'

Bingwen was staring at the woodcarver's face as if he was looking for the answer to a question.

'We all have family members whom we don't know . . . somewhere Under Heaven,' he said. 'He would have left the family, disappeared.'

'My father was the one who disappeared,' Master Huan said.

'Your father?'

'He left my mother to raise me and my brother. He went away to live—'

'In the mountains?'

The woodcarver nodded. 'My mother never spoke of him again.'

Danzi's old-man shape wavered. Bingwen was asking the woodcarver more questions, but all the dragon could hear was his own heart pounding. Had he misheard?

'That's the man this gentleman knew,' Bingwen continued. 'When he died, he didn't have much in the way of worldly possessions. But what he did have he wanted to pass on to you.'

Bingwen held out a small silk-wrapped parcel. Danzi made a startled noise. It was Chen-mo's possessions. Bingwen must have taken them from him while he slept. Master Huan peered into the shadows to see if the old man was all right, but his eyes were soon drawn back to the mysterious package that Bingwen was placing in his hands.

'Are you sure it's for me?' the woodcarver said.

'I'm certain,' Bingwen said.

Master Huan unfolded the silk and examined the items inside. They weren't much to show for a long lifetime – a gold coin, a small jade ornament in the shape of a winged horse, a tarnished bronze dagger. The gold coin was what held Master Huan's attention. It was more than a year's earnings for a woodcarver. He called out to his wife. A woman appeared at the door with a baby boy in her arms. The baby was the only member of the Huan family not transfixed by the sight of the gold coin in the woodcarver's blistered palm. He was more interested in a strand of his mother's hair that had come loose.

Danzi was weary. He knew that he wouldn't be able to maintain his old-man shape for much longer. He wished Bingwen would just say goodbye, but the young man was showing no signs of taking his leave. He went over to the boy.

'Is this your son?'

Master Huan nodded. Bingwen reached out as if he was going to touch the boy's arm, but then changed his mind. Instead he did one of his tricks. Pretending to pull something from behind the boy's ear. It was a gold coin from Bingwen's own pouch.

'This must be yours,' he said, putting it in the boy's hand.

The boy stared at it in astonishment. He'd probably never seen a gold coin before, much less owned one.

'I can't . . . ' he stammered.

'Your grandfather wanted you to have it,' Bingwen said.

Danzi was puzzled. Chen-mo had said no such thing.

'Do you work hard?'

The boy looked at his father. 'I try my best.'

'He's a good lad.' Master Huan put his arm on the boy's shoulder fondly. 'He's been up all night helping me make these arrows for our soldiers.'

'You're a lucky man,' Bingwen said.

He suddenly turned on his heels and walked out, leaving Master Huan and his family in astonished silence.

Danzi had to hurry to catch up with Bingwen. Neither spoke until they reached the hills to the west of the city. Danzi's mind was swirling. The effort of climbing the slopes sapped the last of his strength. When they reached a cave near the top of a hill he went inside, turned into his true shape and sank down. Bingwen busied himself collecting wood. It was only after Bingwen had lit a fire that Danzi had regained enough strength to speak.

'I cannot believe it. Chen-mo had a son.'

'Two sons,' Bingwen said.

'All those years we spent together and he never told me.'

'Everyone has their secrets.'

'Master Huan was right-handed,' Danzi said, 'but one of his sons might have been a potential Dragonkeeper.'

Bingwen shook his head. 'They weren't. I watched the boy pick up the arrows and the baby reach for his mother's hair. They both used their right hands. Anyway, I thought you said you didn't want another companion.'

'I do not . . . I just . . .'

Danzi barely had the energy to speak.

'You can't fly in this state,' Bingwen said. 'What's wrong with you? Do you have some sort of dragon sickness?'

'I do not know. It must be because I should be hibernating.'

'I thought the food would have revived you,' Bingwen said.

Danzi shook his head wearily. 'My *qi* is low. Without this life energy I cannot fly and shape-change. I need something rich in *qi*. Ginseng root would be best. I am too tired to search for it myself. Do you know this plant?'

Bingwen nodded. As soon as he was gone, the dragon couldn't stop himself from falling asleep.

When Danzi woke, Bingwen had returned and was boiling ginseng root over a small fire. He spooned some of the liquid into a bowl, and handed it to the dragon. Bingwen watched as he sipped it.

'Are you sure you're well enough to travel?' he asked.

'A good night's rest and a little more ginseng and my *qi* level will be restored. I will be fit for flying.'

Bingwen prepared a meal before putting out the fire. 'Tomorrow we will go our separate ways,' he said.

Danzi nodded. The man and the dragon ate in silence, each thinking his own thoughts.

· CHAPTER NINE ·

AN EMPTY STOMACH

Danzi wasn't ready to start his long flight the next morning, or the next. The ginseng root tea had improved his strength, but he wasn't looking forward to returning to the icy peaks of Tai Shan. He could wait another day.

The sky was the colour of stone and offered no promise of sunlight. At other times of the year, the hills would have been busy with shepherds and goatherds leading their flocks from pasture to pasture, but they had all returned to their villages for winter. Apart from the occasional deer or fox, the hills were deserted.

Bingwen emerged from the cave yawning.

'Where will you go now?' Danzi asked.

'To eastern Chu,' the young man replied. 'It's as far away from the Qin as I can get without entering barbarian lands.'

But Bingwen showed no signs of leaving. He seemed genuinely concerned about the dragon's welfare. Danzi didn't object. The young man found mushrooms and edible roots for them to eat, so they didn't use up their supplies too quickly. He caught birds and rabbits. He also amused the dragon with riddles and tricks.

Danzi watched the young man rekindle the fire. 'What will you do when you reach Chu?'

Bingwen shrugged as he sprinkled a few dried jasmine flowers into a pot of water and put it on the fire.

'What I always do,' he replied.

'But you promised me you would find another occupation. You are a resourceful young man, capable of many things.'

Bingwen shook his head. 'Trickery is the only thing I'm good at.'

Danzi was disappointed. He had imagined he'd seen a change in Bingwen.

'I fancy a fish this morning,' Bingwen said. 'I'll go down to that stream and see if I can catch us a nice carp.'

He rummaged through his bag, pulled out a line and a hook, and went off to catch their breakfast.

Danzi sipped a bowl of the jasmine tea and then started to doze. It was natural that he lacked energy at that time of year, he told himself. All other dragons were asleep.

Danzi's stomach growled like a bad-tempered bear. It was hard to judge the passage of time on a cloudy day, but Bingwen had been gone for a long while.

The carp obviously weren't biting that morning. Danzi had an idea. He would turn the tables on Bingwen and play a trick on him. He'd find a spot along the path to the stream and take on the shape of a bush. Then, just as Bingwen was passing, he would turn back into his true form with a roar. The dragon set off down the track, chuckling to himself.

He selected a place next to a large rock. He wondered just how observant Bingwen was. Would he notice that there was an extra bush alongside the track? Danzi spent some time creating the illusion – adding a little lichen, a few berries and the wind-torn remains of a bird's nest.

From his vantage point, Danzi could see down to the rushing stream where Bingwen had gone to catch their breakfast, but there was no sign of the young man. Perhaps he was already making his way back along a curve in the track that was hidden from view. A bird tried to settle in his illusionary branches. He had to keep rustling his leaves to keep the bird away.

Danzi heard footsteps approaching. He got ready to transform at lightning speed to startle Bingwen. Then he realized that there was more than one set of footsteps. There were voices too. Danzi stayed in his bush shape. Qin soldiers appeared on the path, four of them. Two of the soldiers had coils of rope over their shoulders. They were on their way down to the stream. Danzi anxiously waited until they were out of sight. He had to warn Bingwen. He changed to his hawk shape and leaped into the air. Below him he saw the soldiers crossing a meadow.

Someone was coming up the path towards them. It was Bingwen. Danzi was about to swoop down and warn his friend, when he saw Bingwen raise his hand in greeting. He walked towards the soldiers and started to talk to them. They didn't draw their swords or grab him to arrest him.

Danzi couldn't hear what they were saying. He tried to think of other explanations, but as he saw Bingwen pointing up to their camp, the truth was inescapable – Bingwen was leading the soldiers to Danzi's hiding place. The dragon's hearing was poor, but his eyesight was excellent. He could tell from the men's uniforms that they were not ordinary soldiers. One wore leopard-skin boots and a helmet crested with red horsehair. He was a general. The others were high-ranking officers. A dragon captive would be a great prize for them to offer to their king.

Danzi flapped away from the hill in the direction of Tai Shan. He thought he had made a true friend. He should have known better than to trust a trickster. Anger and disappointment struggled with each other in Danzi's breast. In the end, those emotions wore each other out and were replaced by sadness.

The clouds had darkened with his mood. A sharp breeze from the east grew into a strong wind that slowed his progress. Then it began to rain and the wind flung icy raindrops at him. While his scales protected him, the freezing droplets got into his eyes and restricted his sight. After several hours of fighting against the elements, Danzi was forced to give up. It wasn't more than an hour or two after midday, but the earth below was dark. Lightning lit the sky. He couldn't flap his wings at all. He glided as far as he could and then dropped down, falling heavily.

He landed on the side of a hill. On the eastern side, the trees were bent sideways by the wind, but on the other side there was some shelter, if not from the rain, at least from the wearying wind. Exhausted, Danzi crawled to an overhang of rock to wait out the storm. He closed his eyes and folded down his ears.

· CHAPTER TEN ·

A STRANGE SORT OF RESCUE

anzi woke to find himself encircled by Qin soldiers. The points of their swords pressed against his throat. In fact, one of the blades had punctured the soft area under his chin, and drops of purple blood were dripping down his scales.

'That blood's worth more than gold, I heard,' one of the soldiers said.

'Don't let it bleed too much,' another said. 'The king will want it alive. No doubt we will all get a double promotion for capturing such a valuable beast.'

'We should make up a better story,' the first soldier said. 'About how it attacked us and we had to fight it. Don't tell the general that we saw it fall from the sky in a burst of lightning.'

There were three of them. Even in his

weakened state, Danzi was sure he could take them on alone. Then he realized that beyond the ring of soldiers there were more, many more. A unit of Qin soldiers was camped around him.

The soldiers bound his legs. They had no fear of the dragon. Danzi could remember a time when the Qin were the most primitive of the people Under Heaven, who would run in terror at the sight of a dragon. Now they were the most disciplined in battle, the most skilled in metalwork and the most ruthless. Their bronze swords were of exquisite quality. The hilts were inlaid with gold and silver designs. The long, slender blades were tempered with an alloy which made them deadly sharp.

In the late-afternoon light, Danzi could make out a city to the south-west. For all his efforts fighting against the wind, he had travelled less than a hundred *li*. The city was Luoyang and a unit of Qin soldiers was getting ready to attack it.

The Qin camp was peaceful after dark. The soldiers were sitting around twinkling campfires – sharpening their blades, checking crossbow triggers, adjusting the fletching on their arrows. There was a low buzz of conversation and a pleasant smell of food cooking. They all looked relaxed, enjoying their work, as if they were preparing for a festival, not a bloody war.

Only one soldier guarded Danzi. He sat at a short distance, sharpening the blades of his dagger-axe on a stone, not in the least uncomfortable at being near a dragon. Danzi strained against the bonds that held him.

They were just made of rope. He should have been able to break them easily, but he couldn't. He didn't have the strength.

Gradually the soldiers finished their chores, ate their evening meal and settled down to sleep. The fires burned down to glowing embers. Danzi's guard was sitting with his back against a tree, but his head had dropped to his chest. Danzi tried to reach the ropes with his teeth.

'Can I help you with that?' said a voice in his head.

Another soldier came out of the shadows. Even in the dim light, Danzi knew who it was. It was Bingwen, wearing the blue tunic and red cap of a Qin soldier.

'Do not come near me, traitor!' Danzi shouted.

Some soldiers roused from their sleep,

looking around to see where the rumbling sound was coming from.

'It's all right,' Bingwen called out. 'It's just the drummers testing their skins.'

The soldiers grumbled and muttered, and went back to sleep.

Danzi's angry rumblings hadn't woken the sleeping guard. Bingwen prodded him with his boot. 'I've been sent to relieve you.'

'Is it midnight already?' the guard said.

'Yes.'

Danzi knew it was at least an hour before midnight, if not two.

The guard picked up his dagger-axe and stumbled off to find his bedroll. Bingwen sat down next to the dragon and tried to undo the knots binding him.

'I do not want your help,' Danzi said.

'You might not want it, but you need it.'

'I was wary of trusting you before. Now that you have joined the Qin, I do not trust you at all.'

'I have not joined the Qin!' Bingwen said. 'When the Qin surprised me near our hideout, I offered to deliver a dragon to them. It was the only way I could think of to save you.'

'A strange sort of rescue that delivers me into Qin captivity. You were saving yourself.'

'I'm here now, aren't I?'

Bingwen gave up on the knots and pulled a dagger from his belt. He cut the ropes tying Danzi's legs. Danzi flexed his toes and stretched his calves.

'Don't bother thanking me,' Bingwen

said. 'All I ask is that you fly me away from this camp.'

'I'm not leaving.'

Bingwen looked at the dragon.

'If this is your way of punishing me for betraying you . . .'

'Your fate does not concern me. I have to think of a way of stopping the attack on Luoyang. I can not fly off and leave Chen-mo's family to die.'

'Do you have a plan to save them?' Bingwen said.

Danzi let out a huge dragon sigh. 'No.'

'We don't have a lot of time,' Bingwen said. 'If the soldiers find out I have freed you, we'll both be tied up. Or worse.'

'There must be something we can do to save the people of Luoyang – all of them.'

'Danzi, we must leave. There's no way

that we can stop an army of five hundred.'

Danzi shook his head. 'We do not need to stop the whole army. We only have to stop their general.'

Bingwen looked at the dragon and smiled. 'You're right.'

· CHAPTER ELEVEN ·

DREAMS AND
SPLINTERS

'Nice evening,' Bingwen said to the guard outside the general's tent.

The soldier nodded, despite the fact that it was bitterly cold.

'The old man's asleep, is he?'

'Yes,' the guard replied.

'I'm new to the unit,' Bingwen continued. 'What's he like?'

Danzi was watching from a distance, in the shape of a large rock. The guard was more than happy to fill in the empty hours of his nightwatch chatting with the new recruit. Bingwen offered him a flask of wine. The guard took it willingly.

'So where are you from?' the guard asked, after he'd told Bingwen everything he knew about the general.

Bingwen invented a story about a family

who grew cabbages in the foothills of Qin. The guard yawned widely and fell asleep.

Danzi stepped out of the darkness. 'Do your stories always send people to sleep?'

'A few leaves of a certain herb sprinkled in the wine did the trick.' Bingwen smiled. 'I think we have all the information we need.'

Danzi crept into the general's tent. His dragon eyes could see that it was furnished with a carpet, some cushions, a writing table and an open chest. Danzi looked down at the sleeping general. He was a man of about fifty years. He lay on a thick mattress and was covered with a quilt of silk wadding. Outside, the soldiers slept on bamboo mats beneath thin blankets. The dragon shape-changed.

Bingwen entered the tent, holding an

oil lamp. He nodded in approval at Danzi's new shape – a woman about the same age as the general.

'He sleeps soundly for a man about to order the slaughter of an entire city,' Danzi said.

Bingwen smiled. 'Not for long.'

Their words, spoken only in their minds, didn't disturb the general. Bingwen placed the lamp on the writing table. Then he tucked the general's quilt tightly under his mattress, before crouching behind the chest. Danzi admired his speed and stealth. He could tell it wasn't the first time the trickster had crept around a sleeping person at night.

'Are you ready?' Bingwen said.

The dragon nodded.

Bingwen started to sing softly. His song

didn't have words, just mournful sounds. The general stirred. He opened his eyes. Bingwen threw powder into the lamp oil and the flame began to burn with a flickering purplish flame. When the general saw the woman in his tent, he called the guard. There was no response.

The woman was faint, and had a greenish tinge. She had a thin veil drawn across her face. 'My husband must be dead.' It was Bingwen who spoke, but his voice was high-pitched, and somehow he made it appear to come from the woman. 'It has been so long since I heard from him.'

'Meizhu?' the general whispered in fear and astonishment. 'Is that you?'

The woman stared ahead as if she couldn't see the general. 'Almost five years without a word.'

'But I've written letters,' the general said. 'Didn't you receive them?'

'My daughters have married and left home. The life of a soldier's wife is a lonely one.'

'I will send a message to my sister. She will keep you company.'

'There is a minister who calls on me. He says it is his duty to check on the families of officers.' The woman smiled. 'I think his interest in me is more personal. He says that if my husband does not return before spring, he will declare him dead.'

'No!' The commander tried to get up from his bed, but the tight quilt wouldn't allow him.

Bingwen held a thick piece of cloth in front of the lamp flame. The tent went dark. There was no sound.

'Guard!' he called. 'Did you hear voices?'

'No, Sir,' said a voice. It was Bingwen again, making his voice appear to come from outside. 'You must have had a dream.'

The general settled down. When he was asleep again, Bingwen uncovered the lamp. Danzi had taken on a different shape. This time he was an old man with wild, white hair and a tattered gown. Bingwen put his hands to his lips and made an eerie sound like a wind whistling through trees.

'My son is not tending my tomb!' Bingwen spoke in the voice of an old man. 'He is the head of the family, but he does not give me what I need.'

The general was awake again. Bingwen

waved a fan, so that a wind appeared to spring up inside the tent, though outside everything was still.

'Father,' the general whispered.

He didn't deny the accusations.

Bingwen started to chant:

> *A disobedient son is this father's curse,*
> *But he's doomed to suffer a fate much worse.*
> *When the battle commences in the clear light of day,*
> *He will command his soldiers, but they will disobey.*

Bingwen extinguished the lamp as the general struggled to get out of bed. Finally the quilt loosened. He got up unsteadily and felt his way to the tent flap in the darkness.

'Guard!'

The guard scrambled to his feet. 'Yes, sir?'

'Has anyone entered my tent?'

'No, sir. I'd never let anyone disturb your sleep on the eve of a battle.'

'Fetch the commanders,' he ordered. 'There will be no battle tomorrow.'

The general went over to sit by the embers of the fire. The firelight lit his pale face. Sleep had deserted him.

The guard saw Bingwen come out of the tent, but kept his mouth shut. He would be punished if he admitted that he had fallen asleep. He didn't notice the bat that flew out behind Bingwen.

'I don't think he will fight tomorrow,' Bingwen said as they left the camp behind them. 'We can leave now.'

The dragon sat down on a rock exhausted. 'I may not have the energy to fly,' he said. 'I do not know what is wrong with me.'

Bingwen looked at the dragon. 'Let me see your tail.'

The strange request took Danzi by surprise, but he curled his tail forward. Bingwen counted a number of scales from the tip of Danzi's tail. He lifted one of the scales and reached beneath it. He felt around and then pulled his fingers out.

Between Bingwen's finger and thumb was a large splinter, as big as a child's finger. Danzi looked at it in astonishment.

'Is that a splinter of chinaberry wood?' he said.

'I believe it is. Couldn't you feel it?'

'I did feel a little discomfort but I thought it was a flea bite! All parts of the chinaberry tree can poison dragons.' Danzi was still blinking in surprise. 'How Under Heaven did you know?'

'I just remembered a dream I had last night,' said Bingwen. 'I saw you scratch your tail on a log. I knew you'd got a splinter.'

Danzi could feel his mind clearing.

'You have a lot of dreams.'

'I could never remember my dreams until recently. Now my dreams, certain dreams, are as clear as a mountain spring. I remember every detail.'

'What other dreams have you had?'

'Remember the day we met at the crossroads? I was there because I'd dreamed that I would make a good day's takings at that crossroads. And also, that night we were in Luoyang, I dreamed of a man carving wood. I knew that he was the man you were looking for.'

Danzi stared at the young man.

'Was it a dream that made you come back to release me tonight?' asked Danzi.

'Yes. In my dream you were surrounded by gleaming swords.'

'Your dreams are a form of second sight,' Danzi exclaimed.

'People with second sight are supposed to be able to read the future, aren't they? I can't do that.'

'Second sight is one of the characteristics of a Dragonkeeper. It can take many different forms. Chen-mo's second sight came as visions that blinded him to the real world for some minutes. I knew another whose second sight took the form of smells, another who read omens in the ashes of a fire. For many of them, it is a vague sensation or fleeting image that takes years of practice to interpret.'

Bingwen said nothing.

'Dragonkeepers have three character-istics,' Danzi continued. 'They can understand dragon speech, they have second sight and they are left-handed.'

They were still in sight of the Qin camp. Bingwen was anxious to get away.

Danzi had seen Bingwen do many things – write, chop mushrooms, pick up firewood – he had always used his right hand. For the first time he looked closely at the young man's left hand. It was stiff – the fingers were unbending, the thumb crooked and curled under his palm.

'What happened to your left hand?' he asked.

Bingwen turned his left hand this way and that. It moved as if his whole hand was carved from one piece of wood.

'It was crushed when I was a child. My father came to visit me only once after he'd left me with the old couple. I was seven years old and already working with jade. I was showing promise as a carver. Grief and anger had driven Father mad. He was shouting about the family's shame. He snatched the hammer from me and started hitting my hand with it, bashing it over and over again until every bone was broken. After that I could no longer carve.'

Danzi tried to make sense of the horrible tale.

'Is there another dream that you have not told me about?'

Bingwen nodded. 'In Luoyang, I didn't

only dream about where to find the woodcarver. I also dreamed that there was a bond between him and me. He is my father's brother.'

Danzi looked at the young man. He was about to speak when a trumpet blast pierced the silence.

'What's happening?' Bingwen asked.

Danzi took to the sky in the shape of a bat. He hovered over the commanders, who were receiving their orders from the general.

'I have reconsidered our plan and have come to a decision.' A sly smile crept over the general's face. 'We attack the city before dawn.'

· CHAPTER TWELVE ·

BATTLEGROUND

The Qin soldiers responded without question to their general's commands. In minutes they were all up, armoured and armed.

'We must warn the people of Luoyang!' Danzi said.

Bingwen leaped on to the dragon's back. The darkness cloaked them as they flew across the plain towards the dark city. Danzi didn't bother to disguise himself. He landed on the city wall and Bingwen told the startled guards about the imminent attack. The guards could see torches blazing in the Qin encampment. They didn't need any persuading.

'Your army must meet the Qin out on the plain,' Bingwen shouted. 'Or they will slaughter everyone in Luoyang.'

The torches marched silently down the

black hill towards the city. The Qin weren't trying to sneak up on the city undetected. Trumpets blared, drums pounded, torchlight flashed off polished weapons. They were halfway across the plain before the Zhou army straggled out of the city gate. The commanders were youths who looked too young ever to have seen battle. The soldiers were still buckling on armour. Some had no armour at all. Others were barefoot.

Another trumpet blast rang out and the Qin infantry charged towards Luoyang with a loud and bloodthirsty yelling. The Zhou soldiers stopped in their tracks, fumbling to fit arrows to bows, struggling to unsheathe swords. The Qin were close enough for their faces, distorted with bloodlust, to be visible in the torchlight. Many of the Zhou turned to run, only to find themselves cut off by the cavalry that had circled behind them. The Qin artillery launched a volley of arrows. The Zhou soldiers started to fall. Then there was a terrible sound of clashing metal and tearing flesh as the Qin infantry smashed into the Zhou soldiers.

The Zhou army did not have the discipline of the Qin. Their commanders yelled out orders, but the new recruits were easily confused. Their roughly cast and brittle iron swords were useless against the deadly Qin blades, which swept through the air and cut off the heads of Zhou soldiers as easily as slicing through ripe peaches.

The Qin armour was superior as well, made of metal plates laced together and reaching down to the knees. Even when a Zhou soldier did manage to land a blow, it couldn't penetrate the armour. The Zhou's leather armour only protected them to the waist.

The air was full of screams – the inhuman battle cry of bloodthirsty men and the anguish of the wounded who knew they were about to die.

Danzi watched from the city walls. The huge crossbow was unmanned. In their hurry, the Zhou had forgotten to use it. Danzi didn't know what to do. Once the Qin had defeated the feeble Zhou army, they would attack the city. Luoyang would end up like Gaoping. Danzi couldn't just watch the slaughter. What shape could he take that would frighten these bloodthirsty soldiers?

'You don't have to shape-change into anything,' Bingwen said.

Danzi was so used to hiding his dragon

shape from humans, he had forgotten how fierce and frightening he could look. Bingwen had changed his clothes. He was wearing a white silk gown and he had untied his hair. He explained his plan to the dragon.

'The sight of a roaring dragon transporting an Immortal from Heaven will get their attention.'

Bingwen climbed on to the dragon's back and they took off and swooped over the battlefield. It was terrible to see so much violence, horrible to hear so many screams of agony. Danzi cried out in anguish. The sound of copper bowls clashing together rang out over the battlefield.

The first light of day brightened the horizon. The undersides of the clouds turned deep red. The soldiers looked up and saw an angry dragon flying above them. His huge teeth were bared, his talons ready to attack. Qin and Zhou soldiers alike stopped fighting and covered their heads as the roaring dragon swooped low over them.

The battle noise died. The sky near the horizon had turned pink. The soldiers stood staring up at them. Danzi looked over his shoulder. Bingwen wasn't sitting on his back; he was standing. His hair streamed out. His gown billowed around him, shining like gold in the early-morning light. A terrified cry swept through the soldiers as they saw Bingwen for the first time. Danzi hovered above them.

'Heaven is angry at this violence that has disturbed the peace of the night,' Bingwen shouted.

The wind was in their favour and carried

his voice to the stunned men. Some fell to their knees in prayer, believing they had been visited by an Immortal.

A sliver of bright orange appeared on the horizon, like a luminous strip of tangerine rind. Rays of sunlight speared out from the horizon and warmed Danzi. He glided over the kneeling armies, keeping aloft with an occasional flap of his wings. He hovered above the Qin general, who was staring up from the back of his war chariot. Bingwen pointed directly at him, yelling threats of eternal torture if the general did not stop the battle.

The general ordered a retreat. Danzi and Bingwen circled above as they watched the armies withdraw, the Zhou hauling their dead with them. Some of the Qin collected up the decapitated heads. They were not so frightened that they had forgotten about promotion. Soon there was nothing left of the battle but trampled, bloodstained grass.

The sun had pulled away from the horizon. Danzi flew off to the south. He breathed in the brilliant *qi*-rich light, feeling it strengthen his muscles and bones, enrich his blood and brighten his mind. He felt as if he could fly forever.

'We saved lives here,' Bingwen said, as he sat astride the dragon, 'but the Qin will return.'

'I hope the Zhou will have time to train a better army before the next attack.'

'Or else realize that the Qin are unstoppable and their best course is to surrender.'

'We worked well together,' Bingwen said.

'It was just trickery,' Danzi replied.

'But I've learned how to use it for good.'

'You know I have decided not to take another Dragonkeeper.'

'Danzi, it's obvious that you need someone to look after you. You've only been alone for a week or two and look at the state you've got yourself into!'

'But . . .'

'There's no point in resisting. I have the three characteristics. I am your Dragon-keeper, whether you like it or not.'

The dawn colours had faded, leaving the sky a brilliant blue.

'This is all that my grandfather left me. Father tried to hide it from me, but I found it of course.'

He pulled something from his sleeve. It was a dragon scale, old and faded to grey.

'My grandfather visited me in secret from time to time when I was a child. I dream of him often.'

'And in these dreams, are there . . . ?'

'Dragons?' Bingwen smiled. 'Yes, there are always dragons. All my life I have dreamed of flying on a dragon's back.'

GLOSSARY

CAMPHOR TREE
An evergreen tree that has fragrant wood and is native to Asia.

CASH
A Chinese copper coin with a square hole in the middle so that a number of them can be strung together.

CHANG
A measure of distance equal to about 2.3 metres.

CHINABERRY TREE
A deciduous tree with large yellow berries native to Asia and Australia.

FLETCHING
The feathers on the end of an arrow that make it fly well.

GINSENG
A plant whose roots are used medicinally in China and believed to have energy-giving properties.

JADE
A semiprecious stone also known as nephrite. Its colour varies from green to white.

JUJUBE
Another name for the fruit known as Chinese date.

LI
A measure of distance equal to about half a kilometre.

PANGOLIN
An animal found in Africa and Asia that has a scaly skin, a long snout and eats ants.

QI
According to traditional Chinese beliefs, qi is the life energy that flows through us and controls the workings of the body.

SOULS
In ancient China, people believed that everyone had two souls. One went straight to Heaven after death, the other stayed near the grave. It was the duty of a dead person's family to provide a good grave with food and comforts for the body in the afterlife. If they did this, the earth-bound soul was content. But if they didn't, the soul became an angry ghost.

PRONUNCIATION

The Chinese words and names in this book are written in pinyin, which is the official way of writing Chinese words using the English alphabet. The words aren't always pronounced the way you'd think. This guide will help you pronounce them correctly.

Chen-mo	Ch'n (pronounced almost as if the e wasn't there, like the end of 'kitchen') mow (rhymes with dough)
Chu	Chew
Danzi	Dan za
Gaoping	Gow (rhymes with now) ping
Huan	Hw-an
Lu	Loo
Luoyang	Lw-oi ang (rhymes with bang)
Meizhu	May-ju
Qin	Chin

Tai Shan	Tie shan (rhymes with ran)
Wei	Way
Zhou	Joe

THE DRAGON
ALPHABET

INTRODUCTION

Chinese dragons like Danzi are strange and complicated beasts with a history that goes back more than six thousand years. The shape of these dragons of the East is similar to the dragons of the West – they all have scales, tails and talons. But that's where the similarities end. The personalities, capabilities and stories of Chinese dragons are completely different to those of the fire-breathing monsters of Western dragon tales.

The big difference is Chinese dragons aren't evil. On the contrary, they are benevolent beasts who bring life-giving rain and good fortune.

I love all dragons, even the nasty ones, but my favourites have always been Chinese dragons. They have scales, tails and talons, like most dragons, but in other ways they are unique.

The first thing I ever wrote was a dragon story. It wasn't a book, it was a script for a TV adventure. Because I love research, before I started to write the script I read everything I could lay my hands on about dragons.

Every time I read 'An ancient scholar said . . .' or 'Long ago it was written . . .' I wanted to know exactly who said what – and when. I searched for the original sources and found Chinese dragons in myths and legends, but I also discovered them lurking in history chronicles and ancient medical manuals, books written on bamboo strips before paper was invented. The dragon trail led back six thousand years.

I kept doing the research long after the

script was finished and the TV programme was made. Dragons became my passion. After years of research, I decided it was time to put the research to use and to write another dragon story. I'd learned about dragons from all over the world, but it was the gentle Chinese dragons I wanted to write about.

That's how my novel *Dragonkeeper* came about. From all the information I had learned, I created my own Chinese dragon – Danzi. One book became a trilogy and now this 'prequel' tells the story of Danzi when he was young.

Now that you've got to know Danzi, I thought you might like to learn more about Chinese dragons like him, so I have written an A–Z of Chinese dragons. In it you will find everything you ever wanted to know about these strange and complicated beasts.

 is for

APPEARANCE

Chinese dragons are beautiful creatures. Like most dragons, they are scaly creatures. They have four legs, but even though they fly, they usually don't have wings. They have branched horns, sharp teeth and a hairy mane and beard. They also have tufts of hair sprouting from the backs of their legs. They have distinctive whiskers, one hanging down each side of the mouth. The whiskers are not hairy but fibrous and can be one metre long.

The body of the Chinese dragon is slender and snake-like, narrowing to a tail which ends in a fan-like terminal. The scales of Chinese dragons can be one of five colours – red, yellow, green, white or black.

ASTRONOMY

People who lived in ancient times looked up into the night sky and tried to make sense of the millions of stars by forming them into the shapes of animals from legends.

Early Chinese astronomers saw dragons in the heavens. They divided the night sky into four regions – the White Tiger of the West, the Vermilion Bird of the South, the Black Tortoise of the North and the Azure Dragon of the East. Each region contains seven constellations. The seven constellations of the Azure Dragon of the East include the horn, neck, heart and tail of the dragon.

 is for

BLOOD

Dragon blood is a powerful liquid. The ancient Chinese believed that when dragon blood was spilt on the earth, it turned into amber. Dragon blood was also an important ingredient in ancient Chinese medicine.

BONES

Dragon bones are ingredients in Chinese herbal medicines that people take to stop them from farting or having nightmares. The best dragon bones are multicoloured, with traces of red, yellow, green, white and black.

White and yellow bones are of medium quality, while black bones are inferior.

Thousands of years ago, the Chinese thought that dragons shed their bones and grew new ones, just as snakes shed their skins. They believed that the bones they found buried in the soil were bones shed by dragons. In fact they were fossilized dinosaur bones, which are still used in Chinese herbal medicine today.

BREATH

Most dragons around the world have deadly breath. It is fiery and poisonous. The breath of Chinese dragons, on the other hand, is useful to humans. These dragons breathe mist. The mist forms into clouds and from the clouds comes life-giving rain.

 is for

CHARACTERISTICS

Chinese dragons have excellent eyesight, but are hard of hearing. They can change their size, making themselves as small as a silkworm or bigger than the whole world. They can also shape-shift into many things. There are stories of them shape-shifting into beautiful women, old men, snakes, dogs and floating logs. The only time they can't shape-shift is when they are angry, asleep or newborn.

For ancient Chinese people, the most important characteristic of their dragons was that they brought the rain.

CLAWS

Early Chinese dragons were drawn with three claws on each paw. During the Song Dynasty (960–1279) the number of claws increased to four.

Five-clawed dragons became the symbol of the emperor during the Yuan Dynasty (1271–1368) and it was forbidden for anyone else to use them as decoration. A five-clawed dragon is known as an Imperial dragon.

 is for

DIET

Roasted swallow is the favourite food of Chinese dragons. They don't usually eat people. However, it is recommended that people who have just eaten roasted swallow don't walk near rivers and lakes where dragons are known to live. If the dragons smell the roasted swallow on their breath, the dragons might eat them by mistake.

Another thing considered to be a delicacy by dragons is arsenic. This naturally occurring substance, often found as crystals, is deadly poisonous to humans.

DISLIKES

Chinese dragons hate iron because it makes them go blind. They also don't like wax, five-coloured silk thread or the leaves of the chinaberry tree. No reasons are given for their dislike of these things.

DRAGON KINGS

Dragon kings are powerful dragons who live in sumptuous crystal palaces at the bottom of the oceans around China and Japan. They are protected by armies of shrimp soldiers, which are commanded by crab generals. Dragon kings can shape-shift into different creatures and spend much of their time in human shape.

 is for

EGGS

Dragons are born from eggs. Chinese dragon eggs are beautiful and look like large precious stones. They are occasionally found in the mountains or on riverbanks.

Chinese dragons hatch eggs by thought. The dragon father calls with the wind and the dragon mother calls against the wind. When the egg cracks the sky turns dark and there is thunder and heavy rain. The baby dragon is very small when newly hatched and looks like a snake or a water lizard.

ENEMIES

Tigers are known to attack Chinese dragons, but the dragons are a match for them. It is only the centipede that Chinese dragons really fear. This is because they believe the insects will crawl into their ears and eat their brains.

EYES

Chinese dragons have exceptionally good eyesight. It is said that they can see a tiny mustard seed from a distance of a hundred miles.

In the famous description of Chinese dragons known as the Nine Resemblances, some translations say the dragon has the eyes of a rabbit, while others say the eyes of a demon. Though a rabbit and a demon couldn't be more different from each other, the written Chinese characters for rabbit and demon are quite similar.

If you look at most paintings of Chinese dragons, they have wide, staring eyes that look quite scary – more like demon eyes than rabbit eyes. However if you look at dragon images from the Han Dynasty (206 BCE to 220 CE, which was when the Nine Resemblances were first written down) the eyes are brown and soft, not scary at all. So both translations are correct!

 is for

FAT

The fat of the Chinese dragon is much prized. It makes an excellent fuel for lamps and the flame can be seen over a hundred miles away. It is also useful for making clothing waterproof.

FLIGHT

Chinese dragons are always shown flying among clouds, even though they don't usually have wings. According to an ancient Chinese scholar called Wang Fu, the Chinese dragon is able to fly because of a lump on its head called a *chi mu*. By altering the air pressure inside its head, the dragon is able to lift off the ground.

 is for

GROWTH

Chinese dragons can live for thousands of years. According to one ancient Chinese source, it takes 500 years for a dragon to grow to full size. It is another 1,000 years before it grows horns, and then a further 500 years before it grows its wings. As Chinese dragons are rarely seen with wings, it seems they don't often survive to that great age.

GUARDIANS

Dragons guarding gems and precious things can be found in stories all over the world. In China, the *fu cang* dragon guards the treasures that are hidden underground. Another Chinese dragon is said to guard the fungus of immortality on the legendary Isle of the Blest. Dragons also watch over bodies of water. Every pool, lake and river has its own guardian dragon. Powerful dragon kings protect the oceans.

 is for

HABITAT

Chinese dragons like to be near water at all times and they take care of these waterways. In winter the dragons hibernate, sleeping at the bottom of deep pools or rivers.

Some dragons, particularly dragon kings, are associated with the ocean. They live in palaces on the seabed.

HORNS

Two elegant horns grace the head of a Chinese dragon. They are branched like a tree branch. An easy way to tell whether a dragon is a male or a female is to look at the horns. A male dragon's horns are undulating, while the female's are straight.

 is for

INNARDS

The internal organs of Chinese dragons have been much valued as ingredients in folk medicine. Dragon brains and livers are particularly good if you are suffering from a stomach infection resulting in diarrhoea. Unfortunately some remedies require that the organs are cut from a live dragon.

 is for

JADE DRAGON

Jade Dragon (Yu Long in Chinese) was the son of the Dragon King of the West. He was a thoughtless, reckless young dragon who was always getting into trouble. He burned the pearls of heaven and was sent to earth as a punishment. When he got hungry, he tried to eat a priest. For this crime he was turned into a horse for the priest to ride on.

 is for

KONG JIA

Kong Jia was a Chinese Emperor who lived almost 4,000 years ago, during the Xia Dynasty (2100–1600 BCE). He wasn't a good emperor. He spent all his time eating, drinking and hunting. However, a legend tells how heaven sent him a present – two pairs of dragons.

A man named Liu Lei got the job of looking after the dragons. He claimed that his ancestors had looked after dragons, but he didn't really know how to care for the creatures. When one of the dragons died, he knew he would be in serious trouble if the emperor found out. He got rid of the evidence by chopping up the dead dragon and turning it into pickle.

 is for

LIKES

Chinese dragons (like dragons all around the world) love treasure, especially jewels. They also like something called the stone of darkness, which is a hollow stone containing water. As is often the case, the Chinese sources don't explain why dragons like this mysterious stone.

LONG

The word for dragon in standard Chinese is *long*. In Cantonese it is *loong*.

 is for

MEDICINE

Bits of a dragon's body were added to potions and ointments to cure all sorts of ailments in ancient times. Chinese herbalists made a medicine from dragon bones that could cure nightmares. A Chinese medical book, written in 1596 CE, lists medicinal uses for dragons' bones, teeth and horns. There are detailed recipes for making medicines for curing many ailments including diarrhoea, fever in children and devil possession.

Marco Polo, the Italian explorer who travelled to China in the thirteenth century, reported that the gall bladders of dragons were used to heal people who had been bitten by mad dogs and to help women who were having difficulties in childbirth.

 is for

NINE DRAGON SCREEN
Screens decorated with dragons are some-

times placed just inside gateways in Chinese buildings. They are there to scare away evil spirits. The most famous Nine Dragon Screen is in Beijing in the Imperial palace known as the Forbidden City.

NINE RESEMBLANCES

According to Wang Fu, a Han Dynasty scholar and hermit, the Chinese dragon has the head of a camel, the horns of a deer, the neck of a snake, the ears of a cow, the belly of a frog, the claws of a hawk, the scales of a carp, the paws of a tiger and the eyes of a rabbit. This description is known as the Nine Resemblances and was written down almost 2,000 years ago.

 is for

OMENS

In ancient China, dragon sightings were usually considered to be good omens – but not always. If two dragons were seen fighting, it meant that something bad was going to happen, such as a flood, a destructive storm or even war. It was particularly unlucky if a yellow or a blue dragon lost a fight.

Sometimes when an emperor saw a dragon, it meant that his reign was about to come to an end. In the year 926 CE, the Emperor Taizu saw a yellow dragon coiling in the sky. It was huge and dazzlingly bright.

The dragon went inside the emperor's tent, and black and purple mist hid the sky. The following day the emperor died.

 is for

PARADES

Chinese New Year is celebrated at the new moon closest to spring (January or February in China). The celebrations include a dragon parade. This tradition began hundreds of years ago as part of a ceremony to encourage dragons to bring rain in the spring. Parading dragons are called *wu long*, or dancing dragons. They are made of bamboo and coloured silk. The dragon can be just a few feet long, carried on bamboo poles above the heads of five or six supporters, or it can measure 100 metres or more and require fifty people to carry it.

PEARLS

Chinese dragons are often shown holding a large round pearl in their claws. Sometimes they are reaching out, trying to grab one. The pearl is a symbol for wisdom, good fortune and immortality.

 is for

QIANTANG

This Chinese dragon had a terrible temper. Qiantang was bright red and over 300 metres long. Qiantang was the brother of the dragon king of Dongting Lake (in China's Hunan Province) and was so unpredictable that his brother had to keep him chained to a jade pillar in his underwater palace.

 is for

ROBES

Because the dragon was a good but powerful creature, it became the symbol of Chinese emperors. Emperors wore long gowns known as dragon robes. They were embroidered with nine dragons – one dragon on the front, one on the back, one on each shoulder and four on the hem. The ninth dragon was hidden on the inside of the robe.

During the Ming Dynasty (1368–1644), the emperor made a law that forbade ordinary people from decorating their clothes with dragons, but dragons were so popular that the people ignored the law. Not wanting to lose face, the emperor decreed that there would be two sorts of dragons – the regular four-clawed dragon for the common folk and a special five-clawed dragon exclusively for imperial use.

 is for

SALIVA

The saliva of Chinese dragons doesn't have medicinal uses, but in ancient times it was used as an ingredient in perfumes. Dragon saliva was found floating on the sea and when it hardened in the sun it turned purple.

It enabled perfumes to keep their fragrance for many years.

The saliva of a purple dragon was used as ink by Emperor Shun of the Yuan Dynasty (1271–1368). He used it only for writing the names of holy ministers and venerable sages on tablets of jade and gold. Emperor Shun's dragon rearer, Yü Hu, collected dragon saliva by holding a roasted swallow in front of a dragon so that its mouth watered. Once he had collected the dribble, he let the dragon eat the swallow.

SCALES

Like most dragons, the Chinese dragon has a scaly body. The scales have magical properties. Each dragon has 117 scales – 81 that can be used for good purposes and 36 that can be used for bad purposes.

Under the dragon's chin there are five large scales that lie in the opposite direction to all the other scales.

 is for

TEMPERAMENT

Of all the dragons in the world, the Chinese dragon is the only type that is not evil. Chinese dragons are good and kind to people. The dragons bring rain which makes people's crops grow. It is only if humans fail to acknowledge this blessing and don't leave offerings that dragons get angry. Then, instead of gentle rain, they bring storms and floods or else they withhold the rain and cause a drought.

 is for

UNDERWATER

That's where Chinese dragons sleep when they hibernate over winter. If it didn't rain in springtime, people in ancient China thought that the dragons must be still asleep at the bottom of pools. To wake them up, they banged drums and gongs. If the dragons still didn't wake, the desperate people threw things that dragons hate into the water –

iron, tiger bones, and chinaberry leaves tied with five-coloured thread.

Dragon kings build their homes under the sea. They are gorgeous palaces which are made from precious stones. The pillars are made of white jade, the stairs of jasper, the couches of coral and the screens of crystal. The beams that support the roofs are rainbow-coloured and inlaid with amber.

 is for

VOICE

Ancient Chinese writings tell us that the

Chinese dragon made a sound like someone banging a copper bowl.

 is for

WINGS

Chinese dragons are always shown flying among clouds, even though they rarely have wings. Some old paintings of dragons show them with wings. In the Han Dynasty (206 BCE to 220 CE) dragons were often painted with small feathery wings.

 is for

XIAN

This is the Chinese word for an immortal – a man or a woman who after death has become a heavenly being who can live forever. Some *xian* are depicted riding dragons.

The most famous are known as the *Ba Xian*, or Eight Immortals. They had an argument with the Dragon King of the Eastern Sea which resulted in the sea boiling. The dragon king's two sons were killed and a mountain was moved. The goddess Guanyin was forced to step in and settle the dispute.

 is for

YEAR OF THE DRAGON

Astrologers use the movements of the planets and the moon to predict the future. Early astronomers named the band of stars and planets surrounding the earth, the zodiac. They divided the stars within the zodiac into twelve constellations. In Western astrology the year is divided into twelve month-long periods, each named after these constellations (e.g. Leo or Virgo).

In Chinese astrology, twelve constellations of the zodiac represent a cycle of twelve years. The Chinese signs of the zodiac are all named after animals (e.g. rat, monkey), but the dragon is the only mythical creature among them.

The dragon is the most powerful sign of the Chinese zodiac. If you were born in a dragon year, you are likely to be energetic, confident and a good leader. Dragon years were 1952, 1964, 1976, 1988, 2000. The next dragon year will be 2012.

 is for

ZHU LONG

In Chinese legend, Zhu Long was a huge

red dragon with the face of a human, who brought light to the dark, desolate north of the world where the sun didn't shine. His eyes were slit vertically instead of horizontally. When he opened them, light poured from them to illuminate the darkness. In winter he breathed out cold, in summer he exhaled heat. His name translates as Torch Dragon.

The first chapter of Danzi's next
adventure by Carole Wilkinson

DRAGON KEEPER

THE EDGE
OF THE EMPIRE

A bamboo bowl flew through the air, aimed at the slave girl's head. She ducked out of the way. She was very experienced at dodging flying objects – from inkstones to chicken bones.

Her master slumped back on to his bed, exhausted by the effort of throwing the bowl. 'Feed the beasts, wretch.'

'Yes, Master Lan,' the girl replied.

Lan scowled at her with the distaste he

reserved for rats, spiders and maggoty meat. The only time he smiled was when he was laughing at her stupidity.

'Don't take all day either.'

'No, Master Lan.'

She slipped out of her master's house as an empty wine jar flew towards the door.

It was a bitterly cold day. Snow crunched beneath the slave girl's straw shoes as she hurried towards the animal pens. The sky was the colour of ashes. It looked like it would soon snow again.

The slave girl didn't have a name; she didn't know how old she was. She had lived at Huangling Palace since her parents had sold her to Lan when she was a small child. The previous summer, Lan had shouted that she was thickheaded for a girl of ten years. As she could only count to ten, she didn't know how old that made her now.

Huangling Mountain was a barren hill in a range of many barren hills that marked the western boundary of the Han empire. Throughout winter it was waist deep in snow and blasted by freezing winds. In the summer the air was so hot it was like breathing in flames. The Emperor's father had built a palace in this faraway place so that the world would know how vast his empire was. Unfortunately, it was so far from anywhere that few people ever saw it.

The palace was surrounded by a high wall of rammed earth. In the eastern wall was the entrance gate. The Emperor's residence occupied more than three-quarters of the palace grounds. The animal pens, the stores and the servants' houses were squashed together in the remaining quarter. In all the slave girl's time at Huangling, there had never been an imperial visit. The palace's graceful halls and sitting rooms, its gardens and pavilions were always empty. Slaves weren't allowed in the palace. Master Lan said he would beat her if she ever went in there. He went into the palace from time to time, but he always came back angry. He grumbled about the wasted space, the unused bed chambers, the cloth-draped furniture, while he had to sleep in his humble house with one room and a roof that leaked.

Compared to the corner of the ox shed, where the slave girl slept on a pile of straw, Master Lan's house was luxurious. There was a rug on the earth floor, and on the wall hung a painting of a dragon on a length of blue silk. The fire burned all through winter and a clever system of pipes carried heat to warm his bed. Even the goat had a better home than the slave girl.

It wasn't the goat that she was going to feed though. It wasn't the oxen, mooing sadly in their stalls. It wasn't the pigs or even the chickens. In the furthest corner of the furthest palace in the empire, behind the servants' quarters, at the back of the stables and sheds, there was another animal enclosure. It was a pit in the ground, a dungeon hewn from the raw rock of Huangling. The only entrance to this pit was a hinged grate, not made of bamboo, like the other animal enclosures, but of bronze.

The slave girl wore trousers that were patched on the knees and too short for her, and a threadbare jacket with many mends. These were her only clothes. An icy wind blew across the courtyard and straight through the worn fabric – even at the front where the edges overlapped and wrapped around her. She looked into the pit, but could see nothing in the darkness below. She slid a latch across, lifted the grate and went down a staircase cut into the rock. The girl shivered. Not because of the cold. Not because of the darkness. Not because of the smell of stale air that came up to meet her from the dungeon. There was something else that she couldn't put a name to that made her uneasy. The pit always had that effect on her, as if there were something waiting in the darkness – something dangerous and frightening.

It wasn't the creatures that lived in the

pit that unsettled her. Even though they were big and had sharp teeth and claws, she wasn't afraid of them. They were an unnatural sort of beast. Different from the farm animals she cared for and, as far as she could see, of no use to anyone. They were dragons.

It was dark and smelt of urine and rotting straw.

It had been a long time since the pit had been cleaned. The girl moved out of the square of pale, banded light beneath the grate and into the darkness. She shuffled forwards, wishing she could bring a lamp. Master Lan had forbidden such a waste of lamp oil. Her eyes grew used to the darkness. The patch of light beneath the grate now seemed bright.

The dragons slept in the darkest corner of

the pit. There were only two of them now. The girl could just remember when there had been four. Lao Ma, the old woman who kept the palace clean, could remember the day the dragons first arrived. She had been no more than a girl herself. Lao Ma said there were a dozen or more of the creatures then. The slave girl wondered what had happened to all the others.

The creatures didn't move as she approached. They had never tried to hurt her, but she had a feeling that they were hiding their true nature. The painting of the dragon in Master Lan's house showed a magnificent golden creature, snaking and shimmering among clouds. In the dim light of the pit it was hard to make out exactly what the two imperial dragons looked like. They certainly weren't magnificent. They looked dull and grey. Their scales did not shimmer. They did not fly. Their long scaly bodies lay all day, curled up like piles of thick rope, in the dirty straw.

Master Lan was the Imperial Dragon-keeper. His seal of office hung from his waist by a length of greasy ribbon. It was a rectangle of white jade with characters cut into one end and a carving of a dragon on the other. It was Master Lan's job to feed and care for the imperial dragons. The girl was just supposed to feed the farm animals and take care of Master Lan's personal needs – cooking his meals, mending his worn silk robes, keeping his house clean. But the Dragonkeeper was lazy. As the girl had grown older, he'd given her more and more of his duties. He spent more and more of his days lying on his bed, eating, drinking wine and complaining.

It was the Emperor's fault, he said. The imperial dragons really belonged at the imperial palace in Chang'an. That's how it had been for thousands of years. A shaman should examine them daily, divining the Emperor's future from the dragons' behaviour. If the dragons frolicked happily in the pleasure gardens, it was a good sign for the empire. If they sulked and didn't eat, it was a bad omen. Many years ago, one of the dragons had bitten an emperor, the father of the current emperor, when he was a child. The child was scared of the beasts. As soon as he came to power, he had sent the dragons as far away as possible – to Huangling Mountain. There wasn't a day went by that Master Lan didn't complain that he should have been at Chang'an.

The slave girl put down the bowl of mashed taro and millet she had prepared for the dragons.

'Dinner time,' she said.

One dragon stirred. She could barely make out its shape. It lifted its snout to sniff the food, then turned its head away.

'Ungrateful beast,' she muttered.

The bowl of food she had left that morning was still there, untouched apart from where rats had nibbled around the edge.

The slave girl had been feeding the dragons since Master Lan had decided he had bad knees and couldn't climb up and down the dungeon stairs every day. That must have been nearly a year ago. The oxen mooed whenever she went near their shed. The goat wagged its tail when she fed it. Even the chickens fluttered expectantly when she brought them food. The dragons had barely glanced at her in all that time.

'I was going to change your straw,' she grumbled. 'But now you can wait.'

She picked up the bowl of fresh food. No point in wasting it on such surly beasts. They could finish the morning's mash first.

There was a rustle in the straw. A nose poked out. It sniffed the air. Beneath the nose were two large yellow teeth. The nose was followed by a brown head, a fat furry body and, finally, a long tail.

The girl's frown turned to a smile. 'Is that you, Hua?'

It was a large rat. She picked it up and hugged it, holding it up to her face and feeling its soft fur on her cheek.

'We'll have a good meal tonight,' she told the rat. 'I've got taro and millet; if I can steal a little ginger from Master Lan's dinner, it'll be a feast.'

The rat glanced nervously at the dragons.

'Don't worry about them,' the girl said. 'They won't hurt you.'

The girl tucked Hua inside her jacket next to the square of bamboo that hung around her neck. It had a worn character carved on it. Lao Ma had told her she was wearing it the day she arrived at Huangling. The girl didn't know the meaning of the character. She couldn't read and neither could Lao Ma. She hurried back up the stone steps.

The slave girl was cooking her master's evening meal in the servants' kitchen when he crept up behind her, startling her.

'I found rat droppings in my bed,' the

Dragonkeeper shouted. 'I told you to kill that pest.'

'I did, Master Lan,' the girl said, hoping Hua would stay still inside her jacket. 'Just as you ordered.'

'You're lying,' her master snarled. 'If I ever find it, I'll boil it alive.'

He picked up the bowl of lentils that were soaking for the girl's own dinner and hurled it out into the courtyard. The lentils scattered in the snow.

He sniffed the stew. 'If there's no onion in my dinner, you'll get a beating!'

The girl hadn't put an onion in her master's stew. There were none left in Lao Ma's food store.

The slave girl ran to the gate. Not the big wooden gates with the bronze hinges which were always locked, but a small gate made of bamboo poles behind the goat shed. Outside the palace walls were the orchard (some stunted apple trees and half-dead cherry trees), the vegetable garden and the rest of the world. Most of the garden was covered with snow, but there was one corner that the gardener kept clear. Underneath a pile of straw, the girl found a few frostbitten onion plants sticking out of the soil. She hacked at the frozen earth with her blade, but it was as hard as stone. She cut off the limp leaves and hoped they would provide enough flavour.

She sat back on her heels. There was a dark orange blot on the horizon. Somewhere beyond the clouds the sun was setting. She wondered what she would have been doing right now if she hadn't been sold as a slave. Would she be happy? Would she be sitting in a cosy house with her parents? Brothers and sisters? Would she have a full stomach?

She'd thought many times about running away from Huangling. It would be easy enough. But where would she go? She scanned the horizon in every direction. There was nothing but snow-covered mountains gradually fading from white to grey in the twilight. There were no villages, no remote garrisons, not so much as a tree in sight. She watched a lone snow eagle glide into the distance and came to the same conclusion as she had all the other times she'd thought about running away. Unless she grew wings, she'd have to stay at Huangling. She got to her feet and went back to finish preparing her master's meal.

After she had served the stew to Master Lan, she retrieved her own dinner from the snow. It took more than an hour of kneeling in the cold and dark to find even half the lentils. She was glad she'd stolen the dragons' taro and millet. Without them, her dinner would have been very meagre. She added the lentils to a pot of boiling water.

A leather pouch hung from her waist, suspended from a length of frayed hemp rope. As well as her rusty iron blade, it contained her secret possessions – a hairpin given to her by the man who delivered to the stores twice a year, a piece of weathered wood shaped just like a fish, and a white eagle feather. She took out the blade and chopped up the piece of ginger she'd saved from her master's dinner. She added that to the pot with the taro and millet.

She went to collect the dirty dishes from Master Lan's house. He was sprawled on the bed snoring. As well as the upturned bowl and wine cup, she took a bronze lamp shaped like a ram from beside her sleeping master's bed. Back in the kitchen she pulled a small clay jar from behind the stove. It was full of lamp oil. She filled up the lamp.

'Come on, Hua,' said the slave girl, picking up the rat and tucking him into her jacket. 'While we're waiting for our dinner to cook, let's go and explore the world.'

Master Lan would have beat her if he found out that every time she lit a lamp for him, she saved a little of the oil for herself. She took no more than a drop or two each night, but slowly she collected enough to fill a lamp.

Outside she shielded the lamp with her jacket, just in case any of the other palace staff were around. It was very unlikely. The men were all as old as Lao Ma. They liked to be tucked in bed early. The girl ducked through a hole in the tangled vine that shielded the palace from the servants' quarters, the animal sheds and other unsightly buildings. It also hid her secret visits to the palace from the other servants. She glanced up at the dark sky. She hoped the clouds would hide her from the gods. She walked through the dark gardens and opened the door of the Jade Flower Hall. The lamp lit a small circle of light on the floor. She followed a dark corridor. This was her secret pleasure, exploring the palace while everyone else was sleeping.

Master Lan was always saying that Huangling was tiny compared to the palaces in Chang'an, but to the slave girl it seemed huge. Each time she went on one of her night-time excursions to the palace, she visited a different room. Once she had gone into the Emperor's own chamber. She had even dared to sit on his bed, which was as big as a wheat field. This time she went to a small hall where the palace women, if there had been any, would normally spend their days. It was one of her favourite rooms. She held up the lamp. The circle of light moved from the floor to the wall. It lit a painting of a mountain with a tiny building on its peak. The mountain loomed above a flat plain, impossibly high, its slopes scattered with tiny trees that were twisted and gnarled but still looked beautiful.

She held up the rat so that he could see the painting.

'Do you think this is what the world looks like, Hua?' she whispered.

The rat twitched his whiskers.

She shone the lamp further along the wall where it fell on a silk wall hanging. This had a painting of a garden. In the garden there was a lake with a bridge zigzagging across it. The garden was bursting with flowers: pink, blue, pale purple, bright yellow. The girl didn't know the names of the flowers. She had never seen anything growing on Huangling that had such bright colours.

'Do you think there really are such flowers?'

In summer, a few peonies struggled into flower in the neglected gardens of Huangling, but they looked limp and pale alongside the gorgeous flowers in the painted garden. She liked to think that somewhere in the world there were things so bright and beautiful, but she doubted that they really existed.

'It's how painters would like the world to be,' she whispered to the rat. 'There aren't real places like these.'

Her stomach rumbled.

'Let's go and eat,' she said.

Back in the kitchen, the girl made sure that the oil in the lamp was at exactly the same level as it had been before. Master Lan had a habit of checking. She spooned her dinner into a wooden bowl. Then she tiptoed into her master's house to sit by the fire. Hua came out from his hiding place inside her jacket.

'Here you are, Hua,' the girl said, setting down a second smaller bowl of food on the hearth.

The rat ate greedily.

Hua hadn't always been the girl's pet.

She had first made his acquaintance when she found him stealing a chicken leg (which she had stolen from Master Lan). She was furious and tried to hit the rat with a piece of firewood. He was quick and escaped easily. Then she woke one night to find him nibbling her fingers. She determined to catch the pest and built a trap out of thin bamboo canes. Once she'd caught the rat, though, she couldn't bring herself to kill it. She decided that he was quite a pretty creature, with his glossy brown fur, pink ears and whippy tail. She called him Hua, which meant Blossom. She started to train him. The rat responded well. Before long he had become quite tame and was the girl's best and only friend.

When Master Lan discovered she was keeping a rat as a pet, he ordered her to kill it. She had to keep Hua out of his sight. That's when she'd got the idea of keeping him hidden in the folds of her jacket.

She settled by the fire to enjoy the food and warmth in peace. This was her favourite time of day.

'Life's not so bad, is it, Hua?' The rat was lying contentedly in front of the fire.

'We've been out to see the world, we've got a meal inside us, and we can warm our toes by the fire.' The rat rolled over so that she could scratch his full stomach. 'And we've got each other.'